THE KEYHOLE

The Adventures of Toots the Cat

by THOMAS McCAVOUR

To my sister Marguerite (Mugs) Tamblyn

FriesenPress

Suite 300 - 990 Fort St
Victoria, BC, Canada, V8V 3K2
www.friesenpress.com

ISBN
978-1-4602-6526-0 (Hardcover)
978-1-4602-6527-7 (Paperback)
978-1-4602-6528-4 (eBook)

1. Fiction, Fantasy

Distributed to the trade by The Ingram Book Company

Contents

Foreword

Amanda Lynn McIvor was only nine years old when she first looked through the keyhole and discovered Toots. The McIvor family had just moved from the city to live on a farm with her grandfather TC McIvor. Amanda's parents did not think that TC should be living alone. Amanda's mother Cindy McIvor continued to work in the nearby city as a nurse while her father Dan McIvor managed an engineering company.

Amanda had an "Anne of Green Gables look" with a pale freckled face and matching bright red hair parted in the middle and two long braids worn to the front. As the top student in her Grade 5 class Amanda was quick to learn, eager to please, talkative and extremely imaginative. She wanted to become a famous writer and kept a diary of each day's events, dreaming of someday using the material for a novel.

Amanda was a normal nine-year old, experiencing all of the anxieties of growing up. She missed her friends in the city and was lonely living on the farm. Her grandfather TC proved to be a good friend and mentor by telling Amanda stories about his own youth and the adventures of Toots the family cat.

1

The Keyhole

Amanda didn't remember why she looked through the keyhole, she just did, and it changed her life forever.

The keyhole plate was old and rusty, held in place by two matching screws. The door had been constructed long ago by some past craftsman, using three unpainted weathered grey planks of unknown origin. Two strap hinges firmly connected the door to the jamb. It was unusual to have a barn door with a lock, but this door had one. All the other doors in the building were secured with simple latches but never any locks. The room was at the back of the barn on grandpa TC's property. It was an old-fashioned barn, a homely building. The walls were wrapped with vertical rows of weathered grey barn board, all standing like soldiers at attention. The boards had shrunk over time allowing cracks of light to peek inside. On the end of the barn, which faced the highway, there was an old faded sign with the words Drink Coca Cola, only 5 Cents painted in white on a red background. It was the only remaining paint on the run-down structure, except for a few lingering memories of a once white metal roof.

What attracted Amanda to the door was a bright light shining through the keyhole. Amanda tried to pull the door open. The door wouldn't open. She pulled again. It was locked and there was no key hanging nearby. Amanda bent down and looked through the keyhole to see where the light was coming from. She could see a very young cat sitting on a window sill. That was really strange. Why would there be a cat locked in the room? Something was wrong with the cat. She looked through the keyhole again. The cat kept looking in the window. It wanted to get in the house. It seemed to be mewing, but Amanda could not hear a sound. It was just like looking at television screen with the mute button on. Amanda wished that there was a remote, so that she could turn up the volume and hear the cat.

Amanda grabbed an old three-legged milking stool so she could sit and watch what was happening. The cat continued to mew and look in the window. Amanda could see snow on the window sill. That was strange because it was the middle of summer. The cat must want to be in the house because it was cold outside.

The cat was certainly not beautiful. It had tabby markings inherited from its wild ancestors. The fur was a background of silver with black markings. Numerous small spots and streaks broke up the pattern as a means of camouflage. A whiskered white face with striking hazel eyes, a pink nose looked directly at Amanda. The triangular ears stood upright like a crown listening for the slightest sound. Did it know Amanda was watching through the keyhole?

Suddenly the door of the house opened and a young blonde-headed boy came out. The cat jumped down from the window sill and bolted through the open door, looking for warmth, security and food. The door closed. The window sill was now empty and the picture gradually faded away.

Amanda ran to the house to find her grandpa TC and tell him what she had discovered.

Everyone called grandpa by the name of TC. It was just two letters T and C. Amanda didn't know why TC did not have a proper last name, he just didn't. TC was getting forgetful, so maybe he had forgotten his last name. It was a mystery.

As a matter of fact Amanda had so many aunts and uncles and cousins and grandparents that she could not remember all of their names. It was confusing.

Amanda's dad said, "I will write down all of the names for you and create a family tree showing each branch of the family."

Amanda thought that idea sounded pretty silly. How do you make a tree with branches out of names?

"TC! TC! You would never believe what I just saw. There is a locked room at the back of the barn and when I looked through the keyhole, I could see things happening. It was just like TV except there was no sound.

"I saw a cute little cat sitting on a window sill. It wanted to get in the house. A door opened and then a young blonde-headed boy came out and found the cat. It jumped down and ran quickly into the house.

"What do you think of that?"

Grandpa TC started laughing.

"Amanda, you are just like Alice in Wonderland finding the rabbit hole."

"Why you are talking about rabbit holes, TC?"

TC laughed again.

"You have finally found my room, Amanda. I thought that you would never find it!

"The cat that you saw was the family cat. Her name is Toots. The house that you saw was my home in Fort William. The boy that you saw was me. I was six years old at the time. The room that you found in the barn is my room. That room is where I store my memories. I keep the door locked and I own the key."

"But TC, I don't even know what memories are!" Amanda exclaimed. "We haven't learned about memories in school."

"Amanda, let me explain. A memory is just like a short story. It is something that happened to you in the past. A memory can be happy or it can be sad. It can be bad or it can be good. Maybe it is a birthday party which you really enjoyed or the first time you learned to ride a two-wheel bike. Or maybe it's the time you fell off the swing and broke your ankle. Each memory is a little bit of your life that gets stored away in a safe place. I keep my memories locked in the room in the barn. You have discovered my room and I can now share those memories with you. It will be our room. From now on you can enjoy my memories by looking through the keyhole.

"But remember, Amanda. This is our secret. Only you are allowed to look through the keyhole and only you will be able to see inside."

"Wow!" Amanda exclaimed. "This is going to be cool. This is going to be better than television. You mean that every time I look through the keyhole I will see a new memory and you will tell me about that memory?"

"Yes I will, Amanda, but remember this is our secret. No one else can share it."

"I promise not to tell anyone, TC, but can I write the memory down in my diary?"

"That's okay," TC replied. "Maybe you can write a book someday."

"I hope so," Amanda replied.

"Now tell me about your cat. Tell me about Toots."

And this was the beginning of a wonderful period in Amanda's life, when grandpa TC shared his memories about the adventures of Toots.

2
Toots

The trouble with living on a farm was that there was no one to play with once the school bus made its delivery. Amanda waited. Her home was next. The bus driver noisily changed gears and the old yellow bus slowed down and then ground to a halt at the mailbox. The red warning lights were flashing and Gus the driver lowered the guard and then opened the door.

It was raining. Amanda jumped out of the bus with her backpack, ran to the mailbox, stuffed the contents in her jacket and then sprinted to the house.

Gus closed the bus door and yelled, "See you tomorrow, Amanda!" But Amanda was halfway to the house and did not hear him. It was another safe delivery.

It was only 4 p.m. and Amanda's mother and father would not return from work for another two hours. Amanda and Grandpa TC were the only people at home. Grandpa TC was in charge of minding the house and acting as the sitter. He spent most of his day out on the front porch smoking his pipe — which was not allowed indoors — and reading the daily newspaper. Amanda spent her free time in the barn. It was her kingdom. She could jump and roll in the hay, swing on a rope suspended from the roof or fight off imaginary attackers. It was fun, but it was lonely.

Amanda ran to the house, dropped her backpack on the verandah and handed the mail to Grandpa TC.

"Hi, TC, I'm home. I'm going out to the barn to check on Toots."

It was still raining, so she ran quickly to the barn for cover. She was soaked. There was a constant drumming on the metal roof as the rain continued to play a continuous musical symphony. That was the only sound. There was not another living thing in the barn. The horses, cattle and chickens had long departed. There might have been a few mice who had escaped Fluffy, Amanda's house cat, but the mice were all living on borrowed time.

Amanda pulled up the milking stool, brushed a few strands of wet hair from her forehead and looked through the keyhole. She could see an old wicker basket with some baby kittens inside. Amanda counted five baby kittens. She sat and watched as they played together. They were all alone.

Amanda ran back to the house to report this memory to TC. He was still in his rocking chair on the front verandah.

"Hi, TC, I just looked through the keyhole and saw some baby kittens in a basket, but I didn't see Toots. Were they her kittens? Was Toots the mother?"

"Yes and yes, Toots was the mother of those kittens. She was probably taking a break from nursing them."

"But she was just a young cat when I saw her first. How could she have kittens?" Amanda asked.

"My memories get all mixed up, Amanda. This memory occurred much later. Toots had been living with us more than a year and was old enough to be a mother and have kittens. "Now, pull up a chair and I will tell you all about Toots."

TC selected his favourite briar pipe from the rack on the verandah and settled back in the rocker. The pipe was his soother. Fiddling with the pipe was a ritual; holding the soon to be warmed bowl in his left hand, selecting his favourite custom vanilla blend of tobacco, filling the bowl to the rim and then packing it down to just the right depth and consistency.

"Hurry up, TC." Amanda was becoming impatient, but she knew from past experience that TC could not be hurried.

TC drew on the tip of the pipe, lit a match and then applied the flame over the tobacco. He puffed on the pipe several times until a red glow appeared in the centre of the bowl. A sweet smell of vanilla filled the air. He cleared his throat and began to tell the story.

"I found Toots one day, sitting outside on the window sill at the back of our house. I had heard her mewing and opened the back door to investigate. That is when Toots jumped down and ran into our house. That was the memory that you saw when you first looked through the keyhole.

"Toots did not belong in our home. She actually belonged to the Handiman family that lived down the lane. But they had plenty of cats and were quite happy to have one less. My sister and I had always wanted a cat. I took Toots into the kitchen and gave her a bowl of milk. She was very hungry and lapped it all up. When I asked my mother if we could keep Toots, she said that Toots would have to go because she was a female cat. She did not want a female cat and a house full of kittens. My grandmother came to the rescue. She convinced my mother that female cats were much friendlier and less trouble than boy cats or toms as she called them. My mother replied that having no cats in the house would be even less trouble. At the end of the discussion, Toots was allowed to stay."

"I was wondering, TC. What kind of a cat was Toots?"

"I think that Toots would be called a grey, short hair tabby cat. She certainly wasn't a pure bred tabby. She was a barnyard cat. She was a mixture."

"What do you mean, TC?"

"I mean that her mother was probably a tabby cat, but her father belonged to a different breed," TC replied.

"Tabby cats have particular markings on their coats. Toots' coat was a grey colour with traces of white and distinct black markings. There were three dark stripes down her back with an oyster shape on the sides and a butterfly mark on the back of her neck. There were clear markings around her neck and throat and legs while the tail was ringed all the way down to a darker coloured tip.

"She had a cute face with a white chin and whiskers. Her eyes were hazel with a black centre. I think that the most interesting thing about a cat is their eyes and ears. Can you wiggle your ears like a cat, Amanda?"

Amanda tried a few times and then gave up.

"I can." TC demonstrated by using his hand to twist his ear.

"That's cheating," Amanda laughed.

TC continued:

"When Toots was happy, her eyes were normal and her ears were straight up and perky. When she was angry, her eyes would become slits and her ears would roll up slightly but stay erect. When she was frightened, her eyes would be open, but her ears would be flat. If Toots was petted, she would half close her eyes and her ears would be erect.

The Keyhole

"After I was born, my mother announced that our family was just the right size. My older sister and I were all the children that she wanted. As a result we had an unused baby carriage that became a bed for Toots. The carriage was made out of wicker with a bottom basket and a hood. This was attached to a metal frame supporting four wheels and a handle for pushing."

"What is wicker, TC?"

"I think that our wicker basket and hood were probably made by weaving thin willow branches together into a stiff fabric. It was a very good product and lasted a long time.

"Now, let me continue. We disconnected the basket from the metal parts and then put an old piece of blanket in the bottom. This was to be Toots' home and we moved it to its final location in the basement.

"That is the basket with the kittens that you saw, Amanda, when you looked through the keyhole."

"I never asked you before, TC, but why did you call your cat Toots?"

TC had to think hard about that question. He paused and sucked on his unlit pipe.

"I'm not quite sure, Amanda, but I think that when I was growing up, the word Toots was a slang term that meant *sweetie* or *honey*. There was also a comic strip at the time called *Toots* and *Casper*. I guess that we named the cat with whatever name popped into our heads at the time. Since we liked both honey and the comics, we picked the name Toots."

"Sometimes people call cats *pussycats* or sometimes they just say *pussy*. Why is that, TC?"

"Amanda, you come up with some really tough questions. I am only guessing but the term pussy is a form of endearment or love and when people look at baby kittens they feel good and call them puss or pussy, which then becomes pussycats."

"What about catkins and pussy willows?" Amanda asked.

TC sighed and then continued: "The connection is probably related to the fact that in the early spring, before the leaves appear, the buds or catkins of a willow tree come into flower and are covered in a fine greyish fur, which is just like the fur of a baby kitten."

Amanda was satisfied with TC's answers; there were no further questions.

3
The Amethyst Mine

"Give me a lever long enough and a fulcrum on which to place it and I shall move the world."
— Archimedes

"TC, I was looking through the keyhole and I saw you and another boy looking down a hole in the ground. What was going on?"

As usual, TC was out on the front porch reading a newspaper with an unlit pipe in his mouth. He took the pipe out of his mouth, tilted his head back and closed his eyes. Amanda waited for an answer.

TC opened his eyes. "Sorry for the delay, Amanda, but I had to think back in time to remember what I was doing that day.

"Now I remember. That was the time that we almost lost Toots down the mine shaft."

"What happened?" Amanda asked.

TC picked his favourite briar pipe from the rack and stuck it in his mouth with the bowl empty and unlit. Smoking had been a lifelong habit and it was a hard habit to break.

"Well, it was in the summer and our family was at our cottage at Amethyst Harbour. My friend Mike was visiting and we decided to visit the amethyst mine and look for some good pieces of gemstone to add to our rock collection."

"What is amethyst?" Amanda asked.

"Amethyst is a purple or violet coloured semi-precious gemstone that is found in various countries in the world. Some of the richest deposits were discovered hundreds of years ago near our cottage at Amethyst Harbour. There was an abandoned amethyst mine not far from our cottage and as young boys we would hike over to the mine and search for leftover pieces of amethyst rock."

"What do you mean by a semi-precious gemstone?"

"Semi-precious gemstones are usually easy to find, not as hard and not as clear or translucent as precious stones. Precious stones include diamonds, rubies, emeralds and sapphires, while semi-precious stones would include amethyst, quartz, agates and garnets.

"Give me a minute, Amanda, and I will go in the house and get you a piece of amethyst." He emerged minutes later with a small cloth pouch in his hand.

"This is for you, Amanda," and he handed her the pouch.

Amanda pulled on the draw string. There was a small rock inside. It had been tumbled into a smooth triangular shape. TC picked the stone from Amanda's hand and held it up to the light so that he could look at it closely. It was semi-translucent.

"I was given this piece of amethyst when I visited the Ontario Parliament Buildings at Queen's Park in Toronto. Each visitor gets one as a souvenir. This small piece of amethyst is like our white trillium floral emblem. It is the gemstone emblem for Ontario."

TC handed the stone back to Amanda.

"You can keep the stone, Amanda."

"Thank you, TC, now tell me about Toots and the mine."

TC resumed the story: "Mike put our lunch, two hammers and some steel chisels in his bike-basket and I put Toots in my basket. Toots liked to ride in the basket and she also liked to go looking for mice at the mine. So we headed off on our bikes and followed the road up to the railway tracks. Then we followed a trail beside the track for three km until we reached another path that led to the abandoned mine. We could not ride our bikes any further so we unloaded our gear and hiked up a narrower path to the old mine site. The amethyst was located in a granite fault or large crack, which was formed billions of years ago."

Amanda interrupted: "How did they find that crack, TC?"

"Many years ago, probably when they were first building the railway or perhaps when they were cutting timber, someone found a piece of amethyst that was exposed near the surface of the crack. There is no record of who made the discovery, but I do know that they mined the amethyst years ago and shipped it from Amethyst Harbour.

"The amethyst was mined by digging vertical shafts where the fault was located and then dynamite was used to extract large chunks of amethyst. These large pieces of stone were then shipped to various parts of the world for processing into smaller crystals and then into jewelry."

"Why did they abandon the mine?" Amanda asked.

"Well I guess that they had just run out of good amethyst or maybe there was another location that they could mine easier."

"So how did you and Mike find your amethyst?"

"Well usually we just looked around on the surface and there were plenty of small pieces of leftover amethyst that we collected."

"Did you go down the shafts and explore the mine?" Amanda asked.

"No, that was too dangerous. With the passage of time, many of the shafts had become overgrown with weeds and groundcover. Some were partly filled with water. They were almost invisible. The shafts were usually nine or 10 metres deep and required a ladder to get down. All of the ladders had been removed by the miners or stolen from the site. I guess that we could have brought some rope and lowered ourselves down the shaft, but that would have been pretty tricky. It would have been easy to go down, yet hard to get back up. We would also have needed lanterns because it was dark underground and we needed tools to chop out the amethyst.

"I don't know why Toots jumped, but I think she saw a butterfly that had landed on a patch of milkweed. She jumped at the butterfly and then she disappeared. Mike and I took a close look and discovered that the weeds were hiding the opening to an old mine shaft. Toots had fallen down the shaft. We could hear her mewing for help, but we couldn't see her. It was too dark. We knew she was alive, but we did not know if she had broken any bones in the fall. We were hopeful that she had landed on her four feet."

"What did you and Mike decide to do then, TC?"

"Well frankly we didn't know what to do. Obviously we needed a ladder but that would involve some adult help plus the difficulty of getting a ladder to the mine site. A rope would be difficult to use and of course we didn't have a rope.

The Keyhole

"Can we use a pole or a tree?' my friend Mike asked. 'If she isn't injured she can climb out by herself.'

"I thought that was a good idea, so we both looked around the mine site for a suitable pole. I found an abandoned piece of pine tree that someone had once cut and trimmed. It was about 9 metres long and it was heavy. Mike and I were able to drag it to the shaft. We stuck one end in the hole and then lifted up the other end. The pole became stuck with one end about 1 metre off the ground. We could not move the free end any higher.

"I had just finished reading a story about how they raised the statues on Easter Island using levers and stones, so I suggested to Mike that we should use levers.

"Mike didn't have any better suggestions, so we found another pole and put some flat rocks near the base of the pole that was stuck and then used our second pole as a lever.

"Get me a small flat stick and two flat rocks, Amanda, and I will show you how a lever works."

TC then introduced Amanda to the law of the lever. He placed one flat rock on the table and lay the stick on the rock with a short portion hanging over one end. Then he placed the second flat rock on the short end of the stick. The short end went down and the long end went up. Then he pressed down lightly on the long end and the short end supporting the rock lifted easily.

"That is how a lever works. We could jack the post up using another pole and some stones as a lever.

"The jacking was successful and the post slid down the shaft. Mike and I hoped that we had not killed Toots in the process because we could no longer hear any mewing.

"A few minutes passed. Then suddenly she appeared at the top of the pole. She was safe and sound. With her tail held high, Toots ran to my waiting arms."

"That's a good memory, TC. It's a good thing that you knew about levers."

"You can thank Archimedes," TC replied.

4
Riding the Rails

"We thought it was the magic carpet…
the click of the rails…romance."
– Frank Lincoln Uys

"TC, when I looked through the keyhole I saw three men sitting with Toots on your back steps. An old lady came out the back door and handed them some bowls and some spoons. Then they started to eat from the bowls. Toots had a bowl and was also eating. What was going on? What were they eating? Who were these men?"

"Whoa! Whoa, up there, young lady. One question at a time please. I will start with your last question.

"The men that you saw were called 'hobos'. They were men who did not have a job. They rode the rails. They hitched rides on freight trains that travelled across Canada. They moved from one place to another looking for work. They wanted a job very badly and travelled anywhere looking for work. These men were not like 'tramps' who work only when they are forced to, and they were not like 'bums' who do not work at all.

"These were hard times for many people, Amanda. This period in time was called *The Depression*. It was 1936 and I was only six years of age.

"Hobos were good men. Hobos were usually young men. You had to be young enough to jump on to a moving train. Many died in the attempt, crushed under the wheels. These men were just down on their luck. The old lady that you saw was my grandmother. She knew that they were good men because she had lived during some pretty hard times as well.

"So in answer to your second question, grandma was feeding the hobos a bowl of porridge with warm milk and brown sugar."

"Was Toots having porridge as well?" Amanda asked.

"Well, she did not like porridge, but she did like warm milk. This was unusual for a cat because most cats do not drink milk. She also liked to be with the men because they would pet her and make a fuss over her. I guess that the hobos were lonely and Toots reminded them of home.

"After the men finished their porridge, my grandma would bring out some tea and stale bread with lard spread on the top. Some of the men had lost most of their teeth and would dip the bread in their tea to soften it up."

Amanda made a face.

"Stale bread with lard sounds pretty gross to me. What did it taste like, TC?"

"Actually lard doesn't have much taste. It is the fat from a pig and it is very good for you. There are a lot of good vitamins and minerals in it. I don't think that my grandmother knew anything about nutrition. She just knew that she had lard on toast as a young girl and that it was cheap and better than eating a piece of stale bread by itself.

"Once the men had finished their meal, they would volunteer to do some chores around the house. My grandmother kept a list of 'things to do', which included cutting the grass, weeding the garden, taking out the garbage and picking raspberries. It was fair payment for a good breakfast.

"The hobos felt that they had repaid a debt and my grandmother agreed."

"Where did the hobos come from, TC?"

"Well, Amanda, as I said before, this was a time called *The Great Depression*. Millions of people were without work all over the world. That period of time was also called *The Dirty Thirties*. Few countries were affected as severely as Canada. There was no market for our grain, wood and minerals. The Prairie Provinces were severely affected.

"My wife Shirley and her family lived on a farm near Prince Albert, Saskatchewan. There was no market for wheat and the farms were also affected by drought, plagues of grasshoppers and hail storms. Many of the farmers went bankrupt and lost their homes. Some of the younger people decided to 'ride the rails' looking for work.

"There were job opportunities in the provinces of Ontario and Quebec so the men in the Prairies hitched rides on freight trains carrying grain to eastern Canada. These were the men that you saw sitting on our back steps."

"How did they know about your grandma and how did they find your house?" Amanda asked.

"Well, to cope with their difficult life, hobos developed a system of symbols or a sign code using chalk or coal to provide directions. There was a train track close to our home and the trains would slow down when they were in the city. There were telephone and electrical poles erected beside the track and the hobos would attach their signs to the poles. On a pole close to our home they had posted a sign with a cat on it and the numerals 1416 underneath. The sign meant that you could get food from a kind lady who owned a cat that lived at a house whose number was 1416. The sign worked because there were always three or four men at our back door every day. Toots was always there to greet them."

Amanda thought about this memory.

"Well, I'm sure glad it is not *The Depression* now, TC. I think your grandma was a good lady, to feed the hobos."

TC smiled.

"She certainly was a good person, Amanda, and she is part of your family. She is your great, great grandmother."

5

My Grandfather's Clock

My Grandfather's clock
Was too large for the shelf,
So it stood ninety years on the floor;
It was taller by half
Than the old man himself,
Though it weighed not a pennyweight more;
It was bought on the morn
Of the day he was born,
It was always his pleasure and pride;

But it stopped short
Never to go again,
When the old man died.
Ninety years without slumbering,
Tick, tock, tick, tock,
His life seconds numbering
Tick, tock, tick ,tock,
It stopped short,
Never to go again,
When the old man died.

Henry Clay Work
1876

Amanda ran to the house. When she looked through the keyhole, she had seen a new memory.

"TC, I just saw Toots sitting in front of a big clock watching the pendulum swinging back and forth. It looked just like the clock in our living room. Is it our clock?"

"Yes it is the clock in our living room, Amanda. It was purchased by my father on the day that I was born. My mother was not very thrilled with the purchase. She would have preferred a new baby carriage because the existing wicker one was in bad shape. The clock was about 2 metres high and had a long case to accommodate a pendulum and weights. "Come with me and I will show you how the clock works."

TC reached for his cane and got up from his rocking chair. He and Amanda walked slowly to the living room where the clock was standing in a corner. TC opened a glass door at the front of the clock, so that they could look inside.

"This is an eight-day clock, Amanda. I wind it up once a week, so that it never stops working."

"Why do you wind it up once a week, if it's an eight-day clock?" she asked.

TC sighed. "I guess the extra day is in case you forget. It is also easier to remember to do something on the same day of the week. I wind this clock every Sunday."

TC picked up a key that was hanging on a hook at the back of the clock and showed it to Amanda.

"I won't wind it up now, Amanda, but every Sunday morning I stick the key in the keyholes on the dial and wind up the weights."

The Keyhole

TC stuck the key into one of the keyholes to show Amanda.

"Now look inside, Amanda. It is Thursday so the weights are about halfway down."

"What are the weights for, TC?"

"Well the middle weight drives the pendulum, the left weight drives the striking mechanism that hits the cylindrical chimes and the right weight is for the gong that you see. Now, let me show you the mechanism that sounds the hour, plays the chimes and makes the hands of the clock move."

TC turned the clock slightly so that Amanda could see the back. He opened the back of the case.

"Now get a chair, Amanda, so that you can look inside."

Amanda brought a chair from the kitchen, placed it behind the clock, stepped on it and looked inside. The weights were supported by chains that were wound around three pulleys. The pulleys were connected to a whole bunch of gears, which in turn were connected to the dials and the strikers. It was complicated.

TC looked at the face of the clock. It was 5:14.

"Okay, Amanda, now watch that left striker."

At 5:15 a quarter of the chime sequence played. Amanda was fascinated.

"Wow, TC, that is really interesting. But tell me. Why is it called a grandfather clock?"

TC had to think. "Give me a minute, Amanda. I have to get my brain working.

"Okay, now I remember. A long time ago a man by the name of Henry Clay Work wrote a song called *My Grandfather's Clock*. It was the story about a man who owned an upright long case clock that never stopped working. Time passed, the man grew older and when he died the clock stopped working."

Amanda laughed. "I will have to tell that story to my class and recite the lyrics.

"Now, tell me about Toots, TC. Why was she watching the clock?"

"Well as you know, Toots was interested in anything that moved or made a sound. It might be good to eat. She was fascinated by the pendulum and I am sure that she thought there was something alive inside the clock that made noise and movement. When I opened up the glass door each Sunday, she was always there to see if anything was hiding inside. The only time she ever missed a Sunday was when she had kittens.

"She wasn't frightened when the chimes played every fifteen minutes, but when the gong sounded the hour, she would run and hide. After it was over she would creep back just as if she was stalking a mouse, so that she could watch the pendulum. She just never learned. She never caught the pendulum."

Amanda gave TC a hug.

"Thanks for the memory, TC, and thanks for showing me how the clock worked. I hope your clock keeps ticking."

6
Red Roots

"Hi, Amanda, is this a new hair style?"

Amanda usually wore her long red hair in braids, but today it hung loose. It wasn't completely straight. There was a slight curl on the ends.

"I hate my red hair, TC. I think I look weird. I wish it was thick and curly like your hair is. My best friend Amy has beautiful auburn hair, which she usually wears in ringlets and my second best friend Kate has blonde hair with bangs."

TC indeed had a full head of curly hair, which had progressively changed from blonde to brown to grey.

"You should be proud of your red hair, Amanda. It is very common in the McIvor family. It is one of our trademarks. Your ancestor Jane McIvor had red hair just like yours and she passed it on to the next six generations of the McIvor family that that followed her."

"Tell me about Jane," Amanda asked.

"Well Jane, her husband Hugh and eight children lived in Kilkeel, Ireland. They rented a small, thatched roof cottage with four rooms and a dirt floor. There was one room each for girls, boys and parents. The fourth room was an open area used as a kitchen and dining room. The bathroom was an outdoor toilet and a wash basin. There was no electricity or running water. A peat burning fireplace in the kitchen was used for cooking and heating."

"How did they earn a living and what did they eat?" Amanda asked.

"They had a tough life. Hugh and his older sons owned an open ended yawl with four oars, which they used for line fishing. They sold their fish at the dock. It was a difficult way to make a living and compete with the larger trawlers. While the men fished, the McIvor women grew potatoes in a plot adjacent to the house. With fish as a source of income and potatoes and fish also as a source of food, the McIvor family was able to survive.

"Then disaster struck. A disease affected the potato crop in Ireland and there was nothing to eat. Approximately one million people died during the Great Famine and a million more left Ireland to find work in other parts of the world. There was only enough passage money for two, so Hugh McIvor and his eldest son emigrated and settled in Lorneville, New Brunswick. Jane and the remaining children stayed in Ireland.

"A few years passed and Hugh and his son were able to save enough passage money by fishing for cod and salmon to bring the rest of the family to Canada.

"Those are your roots, Amanda, and there are still many red-headed McIvor descendants in New Brunswick carrying on the fishing tradition."

"Thanks, TC. I guess that red hair is okay, but I still think that I am too old for braids. Now I think I will go and peek through the keyhole and see if there are any red heads in your memory room."

7

The Spud Wars

*"Peace cannot be achieved through violence. It can only be
attained through understanding."*
— Ralph Waldo Emerson

Amanda looked through the keyhole and saw one of the strangest memories yet. TC and some friends were in a field throwing something at some boys on the other side of the field. It looked like they were throwing some small potatoes. Amanda immediately reported this event to TC.

"What was going on, TC?"

"Oh you were watching the spud war. Our gang was fighting the Horner gang. We had spud wars each fall after Mr. Agar dug up his potatoes."

"I still do not understand, TC. What was a spud war?"

"Okay let me explain. Actually it was not a real war. It was a game that we played. It was a lot of fun."

TC settled back in his rocking chair. He had left his pipe in the house.

The Keyhole

"Do you want me to get your pipe, TC?"

"No, thank you, Amanda. Your mother says that I should not smoke so much." He laughed and winked. "I always do what she tells me.

"Okay here's the story. When I was growing up there were only two houses on my side of the street. The rest of the property was used for growing potatoes. In the spring Mr. Agar, the dogcatcher, would bring a horse and a plough and turn over the soil so that he could plant potatoes. There were no insecticides in those days and in the summer he would get us to pick bugs off the potato plants. They were big orange bugs that ate the leaves. He would pay us two cents for one soup can full of bugs. Then we would take the money down to the candy store to buy licorice, bubble gum and black balls. Mr. Agar also told us that we could have all of the small leftover potatoes or spuds after he dug up the big potatoes in the fall. We also had to clean up any mess that we made."

"So why did you have a war using spuds?" Amanda asked.

"Well there was always a war going on in some part of the world when I was growing up and, boys being boys, we always played with guns and soldiers. The movies of the day were usually about cowboys and Indians and always involved fighting. A conflict between the Japanese and Chinese called the *Manchurian War* had just ended but there were still pictures of this conflict on our bubble gum cards and in our comic books. I guess that we were just as bad in our day as you are today watching violence on the television and in the movies.

"After Mr. Agar had harvested his potatoes, my friends and I took over the field and collected all of the small spuds. We invited the Horner gang, who lived on the next street, to come over and help us."

"Why did you call them the Horner gang?"

"There were nineteen children in the Horner family and they were all born one year apart. So there were always enough kids from the one family to fight a war.

"After we had gathered up the small potatoes, we would get shovels and dig trenches in the earth, because that is what you did to fight a war. We dug our trenches on one side of the property and the Horner gang dug trenches on the other side. Then we would create a bomb shelter and hospital by widening one end of the trench and cover it with boards, cardboard and sheet metal. Next we would have a war meeting with the Horner gang to make up some war rules for throwing potatoes at each other.

"First, you had to stand up in the trench to throw a potato and you could not leave the trench. Second, if you were hit on the head by a potato, you were dead and you were no longer in the game. Dying was rare. Third, if you were hit anywhere on the body you were wounded and you had to go to the hospital. This meant that you could not play until the next round. Reporting a hit was on an honour system. The winner of the war was the last man standing."

Amanda was getting interested. "So what was a round?"

"A round," TC replied, "was when you ran out of potatoes. Then we would have a truce so that we could gather up the potatoes for the next round."

"Did Toots get involved in the spud wars?"

"Toots loved the spud wars. She would be in the trench helping us. Whenever a potato landed in the trench, she would pounce on it and then bring it to me. For her, it was better than catching mice."

"Did your gang or the Horner gang ever win a war?"

"No," TC replied. "That never happened. When it got dark, we were usually tired and we would just declare a truce, shake hands and agree to fight another day."

"Did you ever fight in a real war, TC?"

"No, I did not, Amanda. I was very fortunate. I was too young to fight in a war. I was nine years old when the Second World War started and fifteen when it ended. I hope that in your lifetime that you never go to war. I do not believe that you settle disputes by fighting or having wars. I believe that disputes can and should be resolved by discussion and compromise. I hope that you will not only share, but also practice those beliefs."

8

Eeny, Meeny, Miny, Moe

"Eeny, meeny, miny, moe,
Catch a tiger by the toe.
If he hollers, let him go,
Eeny, meeny, miny, moe."
Children's nursery rhyme — Author Unknown

Amanda looked through the keyhole. Toots was in her basket with some baby kittens. Amanda counted five. There were four kittens coloured grey and one was orange. Toots was lying on her side and the new born kittens were all snuggled up in a row, nursing. Amanda ran to the house.

"TC, Toots just had some kittens! Is she going to be okay? Tell me about them."

"I would be happy to tell you about that memory, Amanda. That was the first time that Toots became a mother and she gave birth to five little kittens. I called the kittens Eeny, Meeny, Miny and Moe. I named them like the counting-out rhyme."

"But there are five kittens, TC. You needed another name."

The Keyhole

"The fifth kitten that you saw, Amanda, did not have a name. He was a male kitten and he did not live very long. I guess that I should have called him No-name. To survive, kittens must take milk during their first twenty-four hours. The problem was that No-name could never find Toots' nipple for feeding. He just did not know where to look, so he starved to death. He died shortly after you saw that memory. I put No-name in a small cardboard box and buried him out in the garden. I made a cross using two Popsicle sticks and I stuck the cross in the ground over the grave."

"Did you pray?" Amanda asked.

"I just bowed my head and mumbled, 'Good luck and good hunting No-name.' That was all that I could think of at the time. Toots would have many more kittens during her lifetime and some of them died after childbirth. There would be more crosses in the garden."

"So tell me about Eeny, Meeny, Miny and Moe. What happened to them?"

"When kittens are first born they are attached to the mother with an umbilical cord. This is used for feeding the kittens when they were inside Toots. The first thing that Toots did when each kitten arrived was to nip through the umbilical cord with her teeth. Then she would lick each kitten clean. Licking helped the kittens to breathe properly.

"In the beginning Toots spent most of her time nursing. She would only leave the kittens to go to the litter box or to feed herself. The kittens didn't all nurse at the same time and sometimes they would fall asleep on the job. Toots spent a great deal of her own time licking the kittens and keeping them clean. I always kept some old newspapers in the bottom of the basket and changed them daily.

"At the end of three weeks Toots would leave the kittens for short periods of time so that she could clean herself and use the litter box. If one of the kittens started to cry then she would immediately go back and take care of it. If the kitten wandered away from the basket she would pick it up by the scruff of the neck and return it to the basket. This did not hurt the kitten, because she was not biting into the skin.

"Kittens are not able to see when they are first born. Their eyes are closed and their ears are folded down. By the end of two weeks their ears begin to straighten and their eyes are fully open. The kittens now have all five senses: sight, hearing, taste, smell and touch. The eyes of all kittens are blue at birth, and do not change to their adult colour for many months.

"During the third and fourth weeks, the kittens tried to stand up. Their legs were pretty shaky and they attempted to follow Toots whenever she left the basket. She fed them very little and at that time I started to give them some adult food using a teaspoon. At first I mixed up evaporated milk and water plus a little bit of baby cereal. Then after a few more weeks I added some chopped up fish and gave them some water. Kittens do not need a large amount of food to survive.

"Toilet training began after about five weeks. Toots taught by example. Kittens are very good at imitating their mother. The kittens would follow Toots over to the litter box and she would dig a small hole in the sand to do her business. Then she would cover it up.

"All of the kittens except Moe followed her example and were rewarded with an affectionate lick. Thinking that this was some sort of a game, Moe had a great time digging holes in the sand and then covering them up. Moe was so enthusiastic that he forgot to go to the bathroom. Toots was not pleased. Instead she gave him a swat over the head instead of a lick and then sent him back to the litter box. Moe became toilet trained quickly.

"The completion of toilet training also meant that the time had come for the kittens to leave our home. Most of our neighbours and friends already had cats or dogs. They didn't want any kittens. Our maid Lena came to the rescue. She came from a farm where cats were always welcome. Toots' kittens became barnyard cats and were kept busy in an ongoing farm battle with rats and mice. Toots had already taught her children about the rudiments of hunting by presenting them with a dead mouse. They very quickly learned to be good barnyard cats because that was to be their only source of food."

"Thanks for the story, TC, but I was wondering about one thing."

"What is that?" TC asked.

"Well you have told me all about Toots being a good mother and raising her kittens, but where was the father? There is never any daddy cat in your stories."

"That's a very good question, Amanda. Let me begin by saying that different countries have different rules about parenting and different religions each have their own set of rules. Animals, birds and insects all have different rules. In the cat family the rule is that the female cat is the mother and she looks after the kittens. The tomcat or daddy cat stays away because he does not like other male cats in his territory and that includes male kittens. That rule applies to all cats including lions and tigers."

"You mentioned the word tomcat. Mother tells me that the letter T in your name stands for Tom. Why do we have names like tomcat and tomboy?"

"Amanda, you ask the strangest questions. I never know what is coming next.

"The term tomboy is a nickname that started a long time ago in an adventure story about a male cat whose name was Tom. From that time on all daddy cats were called tomcats.

"The term tomboy again is a very old word and was used to describe someone who was rude and improper. Over time the meaning changed to a girl who acted like a boy. She wasn't thought to be rude but she was thought to be acting improperly for a girl."

Amanda continued with some more questions: "There are other words like an Indian tomahawk or when someone is acting up, they call it tomfoolery. What about those words, TC?"

TC paused before replying: "Amanda, I am sorry but I don't have all the answers."

TC had not only run out of words, he had also run out of patience.

9

Sink or Swim

"A lesson lived is a lesson earned."
— Anon

"TC, I looked through the keyhole and you were sitting by a river or a small stream and you were drying off Toots with a towel. She didn't look very happy."

"She wasn't very happy, Amanda, because she almost drowned in the river and we had just rescued her."

TC lit his pipe and settled back in his rocking chair.

"There was a swimming hole on the Neebing River just behind the tuberculosis hospital. We could easily ride there on our bicycles and on a hot summer day, when it was too warm to play games, we would go there for a swim. Our parents knew that we went swimming at the river and they said that it was okay as long as the river was not flooding due to high runoff.

"The Neebing River meandered through our city and eventually joined up with another river called the McIntyre before emptying into Lake Superior. It did not usually carry much water and flowed slowly. The river was considered to be safe. If there had been a heavy rainstorm, however, the water would rise and flow rapidly overtopping its banks. That was dangerous.

"There had been a rainstorm the night before we went swimming, but my friend Mike and I decided that the river should be okay. We both had baskets mounted on the front of our bikes for delivering newspapers. Toots loved to ride in my basket as long as I put something soft at the bottom for her to sit on. I usually folded up my newspaper bag and she was quite happy.

"We packed up ready to go. I had Toots in my basket and Mike had some peanut butter and jam sandwiches, some pop and a couple of towels in his basket. The river was running full when we arrived at the swimming hole but it had not overflowed its banks. It looked safe.

"The swimming hole was located at a deep spot on the river and there was a limb from an adjacent willow tree that hung over the hole. We had tied a rope to the branch of the tree so that we could hold on with both hands and swing through the air like Tarzan, then let go of the rope and cannonball into the water. It was great fun."

"Who was Tarzan and how do you cannonball?" Amanda asked.

"I thought that you might know about Tarzan. The story is about a young orphan boy named Tarzan who is raised by a family of apes in the jungle. He learned how to swing through the air by hanging on to tree vines. The story was made into a *Walt Disney* movie. So we used to swing on our rope, tied to the willow tree just like Tarzan.

"To cannonball into the water you let go of the rope, tuck your body into a ball, and using your arms, pull your knees up to your chest and hold them there. Then hold your breath, and close your eyes. I could make a great splash. You should try it sometime, Amanda.

"But let me continue. We stripped off our clothes and skinny dipped or swam without bathing suits when we were alone. Mike and I cannonballed into the river. The water was freezing and the current in the river was much stronger than usual. It carried us down river and we had to swim hard to get back to the bank.

"Toots in the meantime sat and watched us. She was quite interested in the rope swinging from the willow tree. She tried to reach it with her paw. No luck. She tried again. It was out of reach. Then she forgot about the river, jumped for the rope, missed and fell in the water. The current in the river carried her swiftly downstream.

"Toots hated the water and hated getting wet. Like anyone in the cat family, she could swim, but not very well. I ran along the bank and jumped in behind her. The current was swift. She got away. Mike was smart and jumped in ahead and the current carried Toots toward him. He grabbed her with one hand and swam toward the bank with the other hand. Toots was cold, wet, and safe.

"That is the memory that you saw through the keyhole, Amanda. I was drying Toots off with my towel. She was shivering and I think that she had been badly frightened."

"Did Toots ever go swimming with you again?" Amanda asked.

"As a matter of fact she did," TC replied. "But she left the rope alone. She had learned her lesson."

10
The Sandbox

"A peace treaty is an agreement to stop fighting."
— Wikipedia

Amanda ran out to the barn as soon as she returned from school so that she could look through the keyhole and see the latest memory. She pulled up the milking stool and looked through the keyhole. Amanda saw a great big box filled with sand. Toots was in the middle of the box and TC was chasing her away with a broom. He looked angry. TC was fixing something in the sandbox now, but Amanda could not see what he was working on. Amanda returned to the house to report this latest memory to TC.

"TC, I just saw you chasing Toots away from a big box full of sand and you looked really angry."

As usual, TC was in his rocking chair on the front porch. He put down his pipe.

"I was angry that day, Amanda. Toots had just gone to the bathroom and had dug up an entire road system that I had just built in my sandbox. The roads led to the battlefront where I had all of my soldiers preparing for a war. She even knocked over some of my transport trucks and my sand observation tower.

"My dad had built the sandbox for me. It was quite large. He filled it with some sand that he brought from our cottage at Amethyst Harbour. I used to build roads for my toy cars and trucks in the sand and I created a battlefront, where I could put my guns and lead soldiers. The trouble was that Toots thought that my sandbox was just another big litter box that she could use when she went to the bathroom outside the house."

"So what happened then, TC?"

"Well the problem was that Toots had been trained to go to the toilet in a small box that we had filled with sand. It was located in the basement beside her basket. She was very good about going to the bathroom. She would dig a small hole in the sand, sit over it, do her business and then cover it up.

"Cats do not do this because they are being polite, it is much more complicated. Cats are territorial. Toots' territory was our front yard, our backyard and the house. Other cats were not welcome. Cats mark the boundaries of their territory by scratching or rubbing against things, to leave their scent and also by leaving their feces uncovered. Feces and urine inside their territory are covered up.

"Toots thought that it was okay to go to the bathroom in a box filled with sand that was in her territory as long as she covered it up. The trouble was that it was also my territory and my toy army could not destroy this cat enemy."

"So how did you solve the problem, TC? Toots didn't know that she was doing wrong."

"My dad suggested that since this was a war that I should stop fighting and sign a peace treaty with Toots and reach an agreement. I thought that this was a good idea and so as part of the agreement, I made up a box which was the same as the litter box in the basement and I filled it with sand. I put the small box in the backyard beside my box. Then I printed out a peace treaty on a piece of paper, which said that I would use my sandbox for building roads and playing with soldiers and that Toots would use her box to go to the bathroom. Each of us would then have our own territory."

"You are trying to fool me, TC. Did Toots sign the treaty? She couldn't read or write."

"Well I asked my best friend Mike to be a witness and I read the peace treaty to Toots. Then I pressed her paw into my black ink stamp pad and then I pressed her paw onto the peace treaty. It made a good print, but Toots didn't like it. She had to lick her paw for a long time to get rid of the ink. Then I signed the peace treaty and Mike signed as a witness."

"Did the peace treaty work?" Amanda asked.

"Yes it did," TC replied. "From that day on Toots used her sandbox and I used mine."

11
The Store

"Everyone lives by selling something."
— Robert Louis Stevenson

Amanda pulled up the milking stool so that she could look through the keyhole. There was no sign of Toots. All she could see was a big old wooden box in TC's backyard. The box had been turned upside down like a lid and was raised above the ground and supported at each corner by four five-foot long wood posts. What had been the back of this box now served as a floor. Some empty wooden nail kegs served as chairs. It was like a small playhouse. The weathered words THIS SIDE UP were stenciled on the front of the box and the words POOLE PIANO COMPANY, with a directional arrow pointing to the front were imprinted on each side. A hand lettered cardboard sign which read Pugmcishin Store had been tacked to the front edge of the box. Another sign, which read KITTENS 50% OFF, was tacked on the side.

Suddenly Toots appeared and jumped up on a counter at the front of the Pugmcishin Store. It was crowded with bottles, vegetables and a large jug of lemonade. Toots was looking down at a basket on the counter. Amanda squinted and looked closer and there were some kittens in the basket.

Amanda ran to the house with the latest memory. TC was in his usual spot on the front porch.

"TC, some of Toots' kittens are being sold at a store in your backyard. What's going on?"

TC chuckled to himself and replied: "So, you have been looking through the keyhole again. That's a really good memory of mine, Amanda. But don't worry. We didn't sell any kittens that day. All we sold was some lemonade and some beets."

"Tell me about that memory, TC. Tell me about the Pugmcishin Store."

TC settled back in his rocking chair and went through the ritual filling and lighting of his pipe. He had developed a bad cough that would not go away.

"Okay, Amanda. It was a warm summer day and my best friend Mike Pugsley had come over to my house after breakfast. We were in the backyard sitting in our piano box shack planning the day's activities."

"What's a piano box, TC?"

"The piano box was used for shipping an upright piano. It was about 150 cm high by 150 cm wide by 60 cm deep and made out of wood. When my mother was a young girl her parents bought her an upright piano. It was a beautiful rosewood piano with ivory keys made by the Poole Piano Company. They put it in the box that you asked about and had it shipped from Boston, Massachusetts to her home in Keewatin, Ontario."

The Keyhole

"Is that the same piano that is in our house?" "Yes it is. My mother gave the piano to me and I gave the piano to your mother. It has brought great joy to three generations of our family. It is now almost one hundred years old."

"Wow! So how did it get into your backyard?"

TC continued: "After my father and mother were married they moved to various cities and always took the piano with them. During each move it was shipped in the box. When they decided to stay in Fort William, the box wasn't needed any more. My father turned it into a playhouse for me, but I always called it my shack."

"So where is the box now, TC?"

"Well it was getting to be pretty old. I guess it has been broken up and used for kindling. They don't use wooden boxes for shipping pianos anymore. They wrap them up in blankets and ship them by transport trucks."

"That's really interesting, TC. But you were talking about your friend Mike. What happened next?"

TC's pipe had gone out, but he still had it in his mouth.

"Let's see. Where was I? Okay we were in the shack planning the day's activities.

"I suggested playing with our soldiers in the sandbox. Mike reminded me that we had done that the day before. He suggested playing badminton or setting up a game of croquet on the front lawn. I thought that it was too hot to play games. We quickly ran out of ideas.

"Just then our neighbour Paul Shinoffski appeared. Mike and I asked him if he had any ideas and advised Paul that we had already eliminated soldiers, badminton and croquet. Paul thought for a few minutes and then suggested that we set up a store and sell something. Paul's father owned a shoe store and Paul said that his father knew all about selling stuff.

"Mike asked what we could sell, but none of us had any ideas. Paul suggested that we could sell lemonade and that his mother would make it for us. Mike then volunteered to get some beets and rhubarb from their garden.

"Paul suggested that we could sell some of our comic books and big little books. I came up with the idea of selling empty wine bottles that we could collect from the neighbours, but Paul didn't like the idea and thought that wine bottles wouldn't sell. Mike cast the deciding vote and said we should try it.

"Then I had a great idea. Toots had just given birth to a new litter of kittens. They were about seven weeks old and could use the litter box. I thought that we could sell kittens.

"Paul thought it was a great idea. Mike was not convinced and argued that since we usually gave the kittens away for free, nobody would buy them. He suggested that we could advertise. He thought that there were plenty of new customers that would buy the kittens and we could sell them at fifty percent off. That was the way his dad sells shoes."

"Excuse me, TC. You mentioned big little books. What are they?"

"They were great books, Amanda. That is how I first learned to read and appreciate the wonderful world of literature. They were big, with 400 pages and a thickness of 38 mm and they were little, measuring about 10 cm by 10 cm. They were very much like comic books, which appeared about the same time, except they had a page of text and the opposite page had a captioned picture. If you flipped the pages rapidly, it was like watching a movie."

"Did they cost very much?"

The Keyhole

"They cost ten cents when I was growing up, which was quite a bit of money for someone my age. But let me continue with my memory. With our inventory planned, we moved on to finding a suitable name for the store.

"A long discussion followed while we tried out various names. This was going to be hard. Finally I came up with the idea of using parts of our surnames. We went over all the different combinations and could not make a decision. Mike resolved the problem by suggesting that the letters should be arranged according to our ages with the oldest coming first. It was in this way that the Pugmcishin Store was born. Paul thought that it sounded like the name of an Indian tribe.

"We hand lettered some signs on cardboard using chalk and then tacked them to the piano box. Stocking the store was quite easy. Mike got permission to pull some rhubarb and beets from their garden, Paul's mother contributed a jug of lemonade and some paper cups, while I had no trouble convincing my parents to sell the kittens.

"The only trouble was the wine bottles. We had scoured the back lanes and retrieved quite a few bottles from the garbage. Our neighbour Mr. Hanigan, had quite a few bottles stored in his garage and said that we could help ourselves. The trouble was that we had to wash the bottles and soak off the labels. It was quite a bit of work but we ended up with about thirty bottles, ten green, ten brown and ten clear. We put these under our display counter, which was by now quite crowded with garden produce, books, kittens and lemonade. Toots had also decided to join us and stood guard at the counter.

"Pricing was difficult. After some debate we priced the bottles at one cent each, beets were four cents a bunch, books were two cents, the rhubarb was three cents a bunch, and lemonade was two cents a cup. The kittens were priced at ten cents each or fifteen cents for two.

"By 10:30 that morning the Pugmcishin Store was open for business. There were no customers. By 12:30 we had fourteen cents of our own money in the money jar after selling seven cups of lemonade. Most of the lemonade was now gone and the ice had melted. Paul went home to get some more lemonade and assured his mother that sales were brisk. He came back with a fresh jug and some matzo bread, which had been left over from the Jewish Passover. We were starving. Mike went home and came back with some peanut butter and jelly sandwiches. I sneaked into our house and got a cup of sugar for dipping the unsold rhubarb.

"We sat around waiting for customers to appear and kept busy reading the big little books and comic books. Paul said that the trouble with our poor sales was our poor location and lack of advertising. We were in the backyard and there was no traffic in the back lane. Paul suggested that we should be out on the front street advertising the store. We made up some new signs which Paul dreamed up. One said Liquidation Sale, which we thought tied in with the popularity of our lemonade.

"Sales improved. One of the neighbours bought the beets, while another bought the remaining rhubarb. Paul went home for a third jug of lemonade. By 4:30 we were all pretty tired of retailing and made up some new signs, which read Free Kittens and Free Bottles. There were no sales.

"Toots was still up on the counter, standing guard and purring happily. Her family was safe.

"Just as we were closing, Mr. Hanigan arrived home and visited the store. He did not recognize his recycled bottles under the counter and ordered two cups of lemonade half full.

I thought that this was odd and then watched as he carried the cups into his garage, took a bottle marked paint thinner from the shelf, filled the cups and then drank them one after the other. What a strange thing to do!

"He wasn't allowed to have liquor in the house," TC replied.

"Gee, TC, that was quite a story. Did the Pugmcishin Store continue?"

"No, Amanda. That was the end of retailing for Mike and I, but Paul did pursue a successful life in sales and marketing."

Amanda had been thinking about operating a store as TC was telling the story.

"You know what, TC. I think that you should have advertised the Pugmcishin Store on TV. That would have brought in more customers."

"That would have been difficult, Amanda. TV had not been invented when I was a young boy."

Amanda nodded and changed the subject.

"What did you do with the kittens?"

TC laughed. "Oh they found a nice home. Our maid Lena took them to her parents' farm and they became mousers."

12
Pig Tails

Amanda was in tears when she was dropped off by the school bus. She picked up the mail and walked slowly to the house. TC was on the front porch as usual, smoking his pipe and reading a book. He greeted Amanda cheerfully.

"Hi, Amanda, how was your day?"

Amanda pulled off her backpack and threw it on the porch. She was obviously annoyed.

"I don't want to talk about it, TC, and I don't want to go back to that horrible school and those horrible girls."

TC was surprised because Amanda was always a happy person and she loved going to school. This was unusual. TC put down his pipe and laid his book on the side table. Amanda could not contain a new flow of tears which spilled down her pale freckled cheeks. TC held out his arms.

"Come here, Amanda. I think you need a hug."

Amanda needed more than a hug. She went to TC and sat on his lap. It was reminiscent of her younger days when TC would treat her latest fall or misadventure by holding her in his arms, stroking her red hair and soothing the hurt. It was comforting. There was a faint smell of maple from TC's pipe clinging to his shirt.

"So what is the problem, Amanda? Why are you crying?"

The words spilled out. "It's those rotten Gibson twins and their friends. Those girls all live in the city and they were making fun of me. They are in seventh grade and think that they know everything. They think that city girls are smarter and that farm girls are stupid. They even made fun of my clothes, my freckles and my braids. They call my braids pig tails and tease me by saying only a farm girl wears a pig's tail."

"And what did you do?" TC asked.

"Well usually I start to cry and then I run away," Amanda replied.

"That is your mistake, Amanda. The girls are teasing you because you are different. You are a farm girl. Be proud of that. You are not stupid, because you have the highest marks in your class. There is nothing wrong with your clothes. They are clean, stylish and well fitted. There is nothing ugly about a freckled face.

"If you remember the story about Anne of Green Gables. Anne had a freckled face and wore her red hair in pigtails. She was teased about both her hair and her freckles. When she fought back, the teasers became friends.

"You must learn to fight back with words and fight back with action. Stand up to the teasers, Amanda. Direct your remarks to the Gibson twins because the other girls are just following their lead. When they do not get a negative response by you crying or running away, they will stop teasing. It will be game over."

TC handed her his handkerchief.

"Dry your eyes, Amanda. Give it a try, I know it will work."

Amanda always felt better after a talk with TC. She wiped her eyes and walked slowly to the barn to check on the latest memory.

13

The Hunter

"The manner of giving is worth more than the gift."
— Pierre Corneille

"TC! TC! Toots just put a dead mouse in your shoe. I was looking through the keyhole and your running shoes were on the back step and Toots had a mouse in her mouth and she dropped it into one of your shoes."

TC laughed. "That was a present for me, Amanda. That was Toots' way of giving me a gift. She was very proud when she caught a mouse and for her, a mouse was a valuable prize. She was giving me her prize because she was fond of me and she wanted me to share in her accomplishment."

"Well, I think that it is a pretty strange gift," Amanda remarked. "I don't think that you would be very happy, if I gave you a dead mouse as a birthday present."

"You are wrong, Amanda. I would be happy, if I knew that you were giving me something of your own, which you prized very much."

"Well, I think it is wrong that cats kill mice and birds. What about the commandment that I was taught in Sunday school? Thou shalt not kill."

"That is a Christian belief, Amanda. There are many different religions throughout the world that have a similar belief. But as human beings we have our own rules and cats have their own rules and dogs have another set of rules.

"Think about it. You eat roast beef and you eat bacon, but a human being had to kill that cow and that pig so that you could enjoy your meal. But it is okay with you because that is okay with your religion. If you are a Hindu living in India, however, a cow is considered to be sacred, so you do not kill it. Some ancient people like the Celts thought that the pig was sacred while Muslims and Jews prohibit the eating of pork."

"Well it may be all right for Toots to kill mice, but I don't think that she should kill birds," Amanda replied.

"Well, what about rabbits, squirrels, lizards and snakes?" TC asked.

"Lizards and snakes are okay but not rabbits and squirrels," Amanda replied.

TC laughed.

"So now you are making up your own set of rules and your own religion, Amanda. You are just like Toots."

"I am not like Toots! But I have another question for you, TC. Where do cats come from? Why do we have cats?"

"There are many species of cats, Amanda. They have been on earth a long time. There are the *Great Cats*, like a lion and a tiger and there are many different *Small Cats* like a bobcat and a lynx. The domestic cat is a *Small Cat*. Toots is a domestic cat."

"What do you mean by domestic?"

TC had become so interested in answering Amanda's questions that he had forgotten to light his favourite briar pipe.

"Give me a moment, Amanda, while I light up."

The pipe bowl was filled with tobacco and lit. Amanda's mother had been nagging TC to quit smoking, but TC was having a tough time kicking a lifelong habit. TC resumed the story about cats.

"About 4000 years ago our ancestors quit moving from place to place and survived by hunting animals. They settled in one place and started to plant and grow their own food. They found that small cats were useful in catching vermin and the farmers took cats into their homes and domesticated them. The farmers also provided the cats with a regular source of food and offered them protection. So the relationship was good for both the cats and the farmers."

Amanda spoke up: "There are cats all over the world, TC. Where did they come from and how did they travel to so many different places?"

"That's a good question, Amanda. I understand that the earliest record of domestic cats goes back to Egypt. The archeologists have found mummies of cats buried in the ancient tombs. The cats appear to be similar to the African wild cat. Traders, during that period, would take the cats on their ships to catch rats and so they spread all over the world. Cats were welcome wherever they went because they could catch vermin.

"So as you can see, Amanda, when you saw Toots putting the mouse in my running shoe, she was just doing what cats have been doing for the past 4000 years. She was just doing what she was supposed to do."

14
The Bat

"Twinkle, twinkle little bat. How I wonder where you're at. Up above the world you fly. Like a tea tray in the sky."
– Lewis Carroll

"TC, I saw you running around in a room chasing something with a fish net. Toots was sitting watching you."

Amanda had looked through the keyhole and had been rewarded with a fresh memory. There was always something new going on in the life of TC and Toots.

TC smiled. "Oh that was the time that we had a bat in our cottage at Amethyst Harbour. Sit down, Amanda, and I will tell you about it."

For once TC did not have his pipe. He had developed a persistent cough and Amanda's mother had given him a lecture about lung cancer. Her most recent lecture had not worn off. The warning was working temporarily.

"Bats are very beneficial, Amanda. We had plenty of mosquitoes at the cottage and one bat can catch from 500 to 1000 mosquitoes in one hour. They certainly made life easier for us. We had a bat nesting box on a laundry pole in our backyard. It was quite high and had a slit in the bottom for the bats to enter. It was facing south so that it would get sun most of the day. Bats like a warm nest."

"How can a bat find so many mosquitoes to eat, TC?"

"They are quite unique, Amanda. They use echoes. They produce a very high pitched sound that we cannot hear and then wait for it to hit a very small object like a mosquito, and then the sound will echo back to their sensitive ears. They can then calculate where the mosquito is located and catch it. The marvelous thing is that they can do all of this in a fraction of a second and then keep repeating it. Our modern day radar works the same way and is modelled after a bat.

"Our cottage was on the North Bay of Amethyst Harbour. It was quite large, two stories high. There were three bedrooms downstairs and the upstairs was just one big open room. That is where I slept. The cottage was uninsulated and since it was a summer residence, there had not been a great deal of care in closing all the cracks and crevices in the outside walls. In short there were plenty of places that a bat could squeeze through the wall for a nice warm and dry nesting place. Unknown to us, they did it frequently. Bats are not attention seekers and they arrived, nested and departed silently. The only traces they left were some droppings. My grandmother constantly complained that I had mice living upstairs, since their droppings are identical to those of a bat. I knew better.

"Occasionally a bat would become confused and find itself flying around in my second floor bedroom with no way to get out. It was on one of those occasions that you saw me trying to catch the bat with a fish net."

"Were you able to catch the bat?"

"Yes, but it took a little time. My sister, mother and grand-mother thought that bats would bite, get tangled in their hair and suck their blood like a vampire. This was nonsense because a bat will only bite if it is attacked. It does not suck blood and I have never known one to get in anyone's hair. The girls were no help. Toots and I were on our own.

"I had found a fish net useful because a bat will fly around and then land high up on a vertical surface like a curtain or drape. Usually I opened up all the windows for the bat to escape, but this allowed more than our quota of mosquitoes to enter. The net worked best with the windows closed.

"Toots was not much help either, since the bats never got down to her level. She was just a spectator and was constantly amazed that mice could have wings and fly like a bird. They are the only living mammal that can do that.

"On the occasion that you saw through the keyhole, I had managed to locate the bat and use the net. Unfortunately I stunned the animal and it dropped to the floor. Toots was about to pounce but held back. She had never seen a bird or a mouse that looked this big. The wing span of this bat was over 30 cm. The wingspans of some large bats are more than 150 cm.

"Look at your own hands, Amanda. Imagine that your fingers and thumb had grown quite long and that the space in between had been filled with a very thin skin. Now put your hands together and spread them out. You have just created a pair of very large wings, just like a bat.

"Toots hissed and backed off with her tail down in fighting form when she saw the bat on the floor. The bat had recovered but it could not take off from a horizontal surface. Bats can only fly from a vertical position."

"What did you do, TC?"

"I went downstairs, got a towel from the bathroom, threw it over the bat and then wrapped it up without injuring it and took it outside. When I opened up the towel, it flew away.

"It was just like fishing, Amanda. I caught and released the bat so it could go about its good work of catching mosquitoes."

Amanda laughed, "It probably went right back and hid in your house, TC."

15
The Butler

"It is important to watch what you eat. Otherwise, how are you going to get it into your mouth?"
– Matt Diamond

"TC, I just saw Toots sitting on a chair in the corner of a room. You and your family were all sitting at a table eating a meal in the dining room. Toots was sitting on a chair in the corner of the room, watching you eat. She looked very dignified. What was going on?"

"Well, Amanda, Toots always sat on the same chair, overseeing the meal just like a butler. She made sure that everything was done correctly."

"Was she looking for some scraps of food?"

"No, she wasn't. She never begged for food. Cats are not like dogs. Despite thousands of years living with us, they are still carnivores. They cannot survive without eating meat. That is why they catch and eat mice and birds. A cat eats just like a lion or a tiger. Cats have never changed. They don't eat plants. A dog on the other hand, is just like us. It will eat anything whether it is plant or animal."

"I have seen cats eating grass," Amanda volunteered. "That's a plant."

"I am not sure why they eat grass, Amanda. Sometimes they eat grass when they are sick or when they want to throw up and get rid of a hairball.

"Cats are also very fussy about when to eat and how much to eat. They like to eat a small amount of food twice a day, usually in the morning and afternoon. I think that we would all be better off if we ate like cats. Fat cats are rare."

"I don't like mice and small birds," Amanda commented.

"But you eat chicken," TC teased.

"So what did you feed Toots when she couldn't catch any mice or birds. Had cat food been invented when you were a boy?"

"There was commercial cat food on the market. Usually it was wet food made from low cost fish and meat, which could not be sold to the public. We used to buy Spratt's cat food. Dried food, like kibble that you get today, was not available. Most of the food that Toots ate was leftover meat and poultry that my grandmother ground up so that she would not choke on the bones. Toots really loved liver and fish. We usually had liver once a week and we always had fish on Friday."

Amanda had the last word: "I think that cats are much better off today, TC. There is half an aisle in our store with cat food and dog food."

16
Blood Brothers

"Blood Brother — A male who swears loyalty to another male."
— Anon

"TC, I looked through the keyhole and there was just you and three other boys sitting in a circle with bush all around you. I couldn't see Toots. I guess that she was not part of that memory. What was going on?"

As usual TC was out on the verandah reading his paper. He had started to smoke his pipe again. There were some dark clouds in the sky. It looked like there was rain on the way.

"Sit down, Amanda, and I will tell you about that memory. It's a very interesting memory. There was a park at the end of our street. It was called Vickers Park. At the end of the park there was a large flat open field. Many years ago some ambitious land developer had surveyed and then laid out a patchwork grid of streets, which were identified by ditches dug into the ground. The streets had never been constructed and there were no houses. As time passed willow bushes had grown up in the ditches. The ditches and the open fields provided us with a great place to play and we spent many happy hours on the other side of the park. Toots would often join us because she found it was a great place for mousing. There was a never ending supply.

"The ditches and the willow bush provided us with an ideal location to build a secret hideout, where we could get together and have meetings. We couldn't use the ditches in the spring because they were quite wet, but for most of the summer the ditches were dry. We built a hideout at the end of one of the ditches near the park.

"As the only boy in our family, I had always wanted to have a brother, preferably an older brother. My three best friends all had older brothers and I thought that it would be great to have someone close that I could communicate with; someone with whom I could share both my secrets and my worries; someone who would help me with my homework; someone who would show me what to do next.

"I loved to read. There was no television or electronic games to distract a young boy in the thirties. Our local library was my refuge and my pleasure. It opened an exciting new world for me. I had read most of the young adult adventure books that were available and also any books that dealt with Canadian history. One of the stories that I read described a blood brother ritual where males would mix their blood, bringing them together into a family. They also pledged loyalty to each other. I thought this was a great idea, particularly since I didn't have a brother of my own. I suggested to my best friend Mike and my second best friends Ron and Jim that we could become blood brothers. They all liked the idea."

"How did you and your friends become blood brothers, TC?"

"We decided to have a blood brother ceremony at our hideout. I borrowed four needles from my grandmother's sewing basket and a small plate from the kitchen. Mike brought some matches and a candle. We all met at the hideout after church on a Sunday afternoon.

"I lit the candle and gave each of my friends a needle. You have to heat the needle first and make it red hot to sterilize it. I had read that dirty needles spread disease. Then you prick the end of your finger and put a drop of blood in the middle of the plate.

"Toots had decided not to go mouse hunting and sat watching the blood brother ceremony.

"'Do you think we should be doing this on Sunday?' my friend Mike asked. 'What does the bible say?'

"I didn't know. Jim the scholar came to my rescue and informed us that the bible says 'that you should not eat or drink blood' but there is nothing mentioned about mixing blood to become brothers.

"Each of us added a few drops of blood to the plate. Then I mixed the blood together with my forefinger and then made a mark on the forehead of Mike, Ron and Jim. I finished up by marking my own forehead with blood. Then I consulted my notes and asked my blood brothers to repeat an oath of loyalty. We spoke in unison.

"'My brothers, we have mixed and shared our blood. Each of us now bears the mark of that sharing. We promise that we shall be loyal to each other at all times; that we shall help each other when help is needed, and we shall share as brothers both fortune and misfortune. Amen.'"

"That was a really cool ritual, TC. Where did you find it?" Amanda remarked.

The Keyhole

"I thought it was pretty good as well," TC replied. "I made it up! My blood brothers never asked me where I had learned the ritual.

"After becoming blood brothers, we decided to go out and hunt for some groundhogs with our slingshots. We had made the slingshots using Y shaped branches from the willow trees. Then we cut a strip of rubber from an inner tube and attached each end to the slingshot. Small stones served as ammunition."

"That sounds like fun, TC. Can you show me how to make a slingshot?"

"Let me finish the story, Amanda, and then you can decide if you want to own a slingshot."

"The Moore house was located beside the park and there was an iron fence that surrounded the property. It was the largest house in town and the neighbours called it the mansion. Large iron gates guarded entry to a well-manicured front garden. Mr. Moore owned three grocery stores and had become quite wealthy.

"We had not been successful hunting for groundhogs and started looking for some other game. We were at the rear of the Moore property. A large black crow had decided to land on top of the fence guarding the Moore's backyard.

"Ron quickly slipped a stone into his slingshot and took aim. He missed by a mile and the stone shot through the air in the direction of the Moore house. There was a sickening sound of breaking glass. We looked through the fence and saw a hole in a stained glass window at the rear of the house. A maid had come out of the house to investigate.

"It was the wrong thing to do, but we ran. We all ran. Of course the maid saw us and yelled 'stop!' We just kept running.

"We had a meeting back at the hideout and decided that we had better tell Mr. Moore that we had broken the window. We put our slingshots away and then walked slowly to the entrance of the Moore house. Toots headed for home. I rang the bell and a maid greeted us. It was the maid who had found the broken window and saw us run away.

"I was the spokesman for the group and asked the maid if we could see Mr. Moore. She told us to wait a few minutes and she would talk to him. Shortly after, Mr. Moore appeared at the front door and greeted us.

"'What can I do for you?' he asked.

"There was an awkward pause and then I spoke up: 'We broke your window, sir.'

"'I know that,' Mr. Moore replied. 'Our maid Molly just told me what happened. Now, which one of you broke the window?'

"I answered promptly: 'We did, sir.'

"Mr. Moore laughed: 'Four boys cannot break one window. Which one of you broke it and I will deal with him?'

"There was silence. We were blood brothers. This was our first test. We all stood at the front door wondering what to do next.

"'Okay,' Mr. Moore announced, 'whoever broke the window has to pay for it and if he doesn't have the money then he will have to work in my store until the debt is paid.

"We all glanced at Ron. It may have been wrong, but he remained silent. Each of us knew that Ron's family had a tough time making ends meet and all of the family members had at least two jobs. We also knew that Ron was up at 5:00 each morning to deliver the morning paper before school and that after school he delivered parcels for the Tamblyn drug store.

The Keyhole

"We remained silent. After all, we were blood brothers. Then Mr. Moore started to laugh and said to us, 'You boys impress me. You obviously are not going to snitch on each other. Usually people are quick to point their finger at the guilty person, in order to save their own skin. But you boys, for whatever reason, chose not to do that. Quite frankly I am impressed. However, that does not get you off the hook. The broken window still has to be repaired and paid for. Now, come into the house and we will sit down and figure out how you all are going to pay me back.'

"While Mr. Moore was on the phone checking the cost of repairs, the maid came in with a jug of hot chocolate and a plate full of chocolate chip cookies. We helped ourselves.

"Mr. Moore appeared with a note pad in one hand and a pen in the other. He sat down and helped himself to some chocolate milk. There was only one cookie left.

"'Okay, boys, here's the bad news. I just talked to Mr. Piper and explained what had happened. He is the artist who created the stained glass window. He said he would do the repair job at cost, if I provided him with a free turkey at Christmas time. He will only charge me twenty-four dollars for repairs. Now here is the good news. I will pay each of you boys twenty cents per hour to work off your debt at the store. That works out to 120 hours divided by four boys, which equals thirty hours each. Do you agree to work off the debt?'

"We all nodded our heads in agreement. The next thirty minutes was spent assigning the various jobs and working out the time schedule.

"Twenty cents per hour was a very generous wage. We had the debt paid off in less than two months.

"I ended up mopping the floors at the end of each day. Mike had to empty the trash bins and take out the garbage, while Jim had to restock the shelves and fill up the coolers. Ron had the best job. He worked on weekends filling grocery bags at the checkout and helping the customers load up their cars. He also made some extra money from customers' tips.

"When the debt was paid off Mr. Moore got us all together and not only thanked us for paying off the debt, but also offered us part-time jobs at the store after school and during the summer holidays.

"To our surprise, at the end of the meeting, Ron stepped forward with an announcement: 'Excuse me, Mr. Moore, I have a few words to say: I shot the stone that broke your stained glass window. But I was afraid to admit it, because I knew that it would cost a large amount of money for repairs and our family does not have much money. We all work hard just to keep food on the table. TC, Mike and Jim are my blood brothers and we all swore an oath to be loyal to each other. That is why they didn't tell.'

"Mr. Moore smiled: 'I thought that it might be you, Ron, because you always work a little harder than the others and I know that your family could use the extra money. That is why I gave you the job where you could earn tips. I understand why you did it and I think that it has been a good learning experience not only for you, but also for me.'"

"That was a good memory, TC. What happened next?"

"We all pursued different careers when we grew up, Amanda. Mike became a lawyer, Jim became a doctor and I became an engineer."

"What happened to Ron?" Amanda asked.

The Keyhole

"Well Ron became a millionaire. He continued to work in the grocery store and he eventually bought the store when Mr. Moore retired. Ron kept expanding and building more stores. He now owns Moore Canada Limited, one of the biggest grocers in the country.

"And guess what, Amanda? When the Moore house was sold, Ron had the stained glass window removed and framed. It is now hanging in his office."

17

A Broken Promise

"A promise made is a debt unpaid."
— Robert Service

Amanda ran into the house.

"TC, the keyhole doesn't work! There is nothing happening in the memory room."

"Then you must have broken your promise," TC replied.

Amanda thought about that and then explained: "Well my friend Billy was visiting and I thought that it would be really neat if I took him out to the barn and showed him the keyhole. I told him that he had to keep the keyhole a secret and he promised me that he would not tell anyone about it. Then when he looked through the keyhole he couldn't see anything and when I looked, the room was dark."

TC was sitting in his rocking chair reading a book. He looked up and smiled, "The reason that you could not see into the memory room was because you broke your promise to me and did not keep the room a secret.

"Remember, Amanda, that you do not make a promise lightly. It is better not to make a promise than to make a promise and then break it. The memory room can only be shared by you and me. The room and the keyhole are our secret. It is ours alone."

Amanda started to cry, but TC came to her rescue.

"I will forgive you this time, Amanda, but never again."

"I promise," she said and then followed with a quick correction. "I mean okay, TC."

18

Lemonade

It was Monday. TC was asleep on the front porch when Amanda arrived home from school. She tip-toed across the front porch without waking him and left her backpack at the front door. Amanda headed straight for the refrigerator, grabbed two lemons from the fruit and vegetable compartment and headed for her bedroom. She locked the door, went to her dresser and retrieved the Skin Care book that she had obtained from the library. It was hidden under a pile of her freshly laundered underwear. There was bookmark placed at Chapter 6 – How to Get Rid of Freckles. She opened the book to check the instructions.

She had already tried the dairy mask which was recommended for natural freckles rather than sun-induced freckles. She had spread a ¼ cup of sour cream over her forehead and cheeks. Then she let the sour cream soak into her skin for ten minutes, followed by rinsing with cool water and lightly patting dry. On another occasion she had used whole milk rubbed into her skin and then let sit for ten minutes. The idea for both treatments was that the lactic acid in the cream and milk peels away the top layer of skin, making the freckles lighter in appearance.

The dairy mask seemed like a good idea, but after each treatment Amanda checked the results in a mirror. The mask was not working. The freckles had not changed. They were still big, brown, numerous and ugly.

Amanda decided to try lemon juice. Lemon juice is a natural bleaching agent that can be used to make freckles look lighter and disappear. The Skin Care book claimed that like the dairy mask, lemon juice works best on natural freckles rather than freckles caused by sun exposure, since those tend to be darker and less uniform in appearance.

Amanda squeezed the juice of two lemons into a bowl and then dipped a cotton ball into the lemon juice. She lay on her bed and applied it to her forehead and cheeks. After ten minutes she rinsed it off with cool water. She looked in the mirror. There was no change. She tried it for the next four days

It was Saturday and the McIvor family were all at home for the weekend. Cindy decided that she would make some lemon pies as a treat. She checked in the refrigerator and there were no lemons. She was sure that she had bought a whole bag of lemons on the previous weekend.

Cindy checked every compartment. There were definitely no lemons. She went out to the front porch where TC was telling Amanda about the latest adventure of Toots. She interrupted the story.

"Excuse me a minute, TC. Amanda, have you been making lemonade for yourself after school?"

There was a pause as Amanda struggled to answer.

"Sort of," was the reply.

"What do you mean, sort of?"

"Well I guess I was using the lemons to aid my complexion. I was trying to bleach my freckles."

TC started to chuckle but Cindy was not amused.

"You mean you used a dozen of my lemons to bleach your freckles? That is absolutely ridiculous."

Amanda started to cry.

"Take a look, Mom. I think that they are getting lighter. I think that the lemons are working. They are better than the milk mask."

Cindy took Amanda in her arms and hugged her.

"Amanda, there is nothing wrong about having freckles. I had just as many freckles as you when I was your age and now look at my complexion. There are not too many and they are faint."

Amanda checked her mother's face and it was true. She felt better and on the following Monday she returned the Skin Care book to the library.

19
Safe Forever

"Safety doesn't happen by accident."
— Anon

Amanda ran in from the barn.

"TC, I just looked through the keyhole and Toots was up a tree and you were also in the tree and there was a fire truck."

TC was on the front porch as usual smoking his pipe.

"Hold on, Amanda. Slow down. I'll tell you all about my little adventure in the tree."

Amanda took her usual place on the front steps.

"Toots had a problem. She was afraid of dogs and would run away if she saw a dog. The dog, of course would chase her. Dogs will chase after any animal that runs away from them because that is the way that dogs think and that is the way dogs act. If Toots had just stood in front of the dog and hissed, then the dog would not have chased her. The dog might even get to like Toots and become friends, but Toots always chose to run when she met a dog and that could lead to big trouble. Toots could usually run faster than the dog and she would run to a tree and then climb the tree to escape. Dogs cannot climb trees.

"We had a big old birch tree in our front yard and it was higher than the house. It was the highest tree on the street. It was a beautiful tree and had been planted long before our house was built. Birch trees are very versatile. Our Canadian Indians used to cut bark from birch trees for the construction of canoes. Birchwood is also hard and can be fashioned into attractive furniture. We always burned birch wood in our fireplace. The bark was easy to ignite and the logs were long lasting.

"Part of our birch tree had rotted where a branch had been cut off. Dad and I dug out the rotten wood and filled the hole with concrete. As the years passed, the wound in the tree healed itself and hid our repairs. I can imagine that some future woodcutter would be quite surprised when his chainsaw hit the concrete.

"The birch tree was also good for climbing because there was one big branch that was just my height and I could grab hold of it with both hands and then hoist myself up. Then I would climb higher so that I could look over the top of our house. I had never climbed to the top of the tree because the branches up there were small and started to bend under my weight.

"Our next door neighbour Mr. Hanigan, owned an English bulldog, whose name was Butch. Butch was short and fat with a coat that was white with patches of brown. His chops were thick and hung down over the sides of a large square jaw. His nose was large, broad and black, somehow pushed back into his head. Butch was just plain ugly. Butch did not like cats and cats did not like Butch. As a matter of fact, I did not like Butch.

"One day Toots was chased by Butch and she ran and climbed the birch tree in our front yard. Butch stood at the base of the tree and barked loudly. The more that Butch barked, the higher Toots climbed, until she was higher than she had ever climbed before. She was even higher than I had climbed and the branches were bending down under her weight. Toots was frightened and started to mew. She did not know how to get down. Butch eventually got tired of barking. His throat was sore, so he went home for a drink of water.

"Toots was making quite a fuss and mewing loudly by this time. A neighbour called me to see if I could coax Toots down from the tree. I got a dish of her favourite cat food from the house and put it at the base of the tree. Toots loved the cat food and I was sure that she would come down to get it.

"The problem was that toots had climbed up so far that she could not turn around and she did not know how to come down backwards. That was the way that I usually come down. By this time a large group of neighbours had gathered around the birch tree and they were offering suggestions on how to get Toots down from the tree. Someone suggested using a long pole with a fish net on the end but there was not a pole long enough. Another suggested an extension ladder but there were so many branches on the birch tree that you could not get close to Toots. Another suggested that we should leave the cat alone and it would eventually figure out a way to get down. But I decided to take matters into my own hands. I climbed up the tree, just like my hero Tarzan, to make the rescue.

"I had never climbed that high before, but there was always a first time. When I got close to Toots, the tree branches were bending quite badly. The minute Toots saw me she jumped and landed on my shoulder. The tree branch that I was standing on bent down even further with our combined weight and my foot got wedged into an adjoining branch. I could not get my foot out and I shouted for help. Now both Toots and I were both stuck in the tree.

"My dad in the meantime had arrived on the scene and quickly took charge. He ordered my mom to go to the house and phone the fire department for help and also to phone Mr. Agar, the animal control officer, to come and get rid of Toots once and for all.

"It only took a few minutes. A fire truck with big extension ladders arrived. They unloaded one of the ladders and leaned it against the tree. One of the firemen climbed the ladder and after cutting away a few branches, he was able to reach in and rescue both Toots and I. The crowd at the base of the tree all cheered. My dad was really mad at me for causing all this trouble. I was in tears. Toots in the meantime was finishing off the cat food at the base of the tree. Mr. Agar arrived and when Toots saw him with his bag, she ran back into the house and hid in her basket down in the basement.

"Dad insisted that Toots must go. The fire department had been called far too often. She was always causing trouble and he was sick of it. I pleaded with him not to send Toots away, but he would not change his mind. Mr. Agar found Toots in the basement, put her in the bag and took her away. The only good thing that happened was that Toots gave Mr. Agar a good scratch that actually drew blood."

Amanda had been listening attentively to TC's story and spoke up.

"What happened to Toots next, TC? I think your dad was wrong to send Toots away and I do not like Mr. Agar."

"You will like the ending of this memory, Amanda. A month later Toots appeared on the kitchen window sill. Somehow she had found her way home Mr. Agar swore on a stack of bibles that he had taken Toots thirty km away to Kakabeka Falls and that she must have made her way home on her own. My dad never said another word about Toots leaving home.

"She was safe forever."

20
Winston

"This land is your land; this land is my land . . .
This land was made for you and me."
— Woody Guthrie

It was Saturday morning and Amanda had slept in. TC was sitting at the kitchen table having his third cup of now luke-warm coffee. He had already read most of the morning paper.

"Sit down and have some breakfast, Amanda. There is some porridge that your mother put in a bowl for you. You can warm it up in the microwave. The milk and brown sugar are on the table.

"What are your plans for the day?" TC asked.

"I've got a ten o'clock baseball game at the park. I'm going to ride over on my bike," Amanda replied.

Amanda retrieved her porridge from the microwave, heaped on two tablespoons of brown sugar and joined TC at the kitchen table. Between each spoonful she asked TC a question.

"When I looked through the keyhole yesterday, I could see Toots up on the roof of a building at the back of your house. It looked like a garage. She looked really angry. Her tail was swishing back and forth and she was staring at a big black cat that had climbed up a telephone pole beside the garage and jumped off onto the roof. Her ears were sticking up and she was crouched ready to spring at the other cat.

"You were not at home yesterday, TC, so I didn't have a chance to talk to you. What was going on in that memory?"

"Let me explain," TC replied.

"The black cat was named Winston and he lived in the house across the lane. He was a really ugly tom cat with a scarred face and only one eye. He lost the other eye in a fight. The garage is a detached building, where my dad kept his car. All of the telephone and hydro wires on our street were strung on poles located along the lane at the back of our homes. The local cats liked to climb the pole beside the garage and sit on the roof in the sun.

"The problem was that cats are territorial. The roof of the garage was in Toots' territory or property and cats could only come onto Toots' property by invitation."

Amanda laughed: "You mean Toots sends out invitations to the other cats?"

TC smiled and shared the joke.

"Cats mark their territory with ether urine or uncovered feces. Toots' territory included our house and the back, side and front yards. The garage and the roof were part of her territory.

"But Winston was a bully. He did not respect anybody's territory. All of the other cats in our neighbourhood were afraid of him. All except Toots; she had fought with Winston on several occasions and he had the scars to prove it. "The trouble was that Toots spent a good deal of time in our house, particularly when she had a litter of kittens. On those occasions, with Toots absent, Winston would climb up the pole and enjoy the roof of the garage. He even had the nerve to claim the roof as his property and would mark it with his urine.

"Toots and Winston were constantly at war. Whenever Toots found Winston on the roof, she would chase him off and reclaim her territory.

"The funny thing was that at night there seemed to be a different set of rules. Toots would allow other cats up on the roof and they would 'club' together and socialize. Winston was never invited.

"The trouble with these meetings was that the cats would often serenade each other by howling. The concert would usually take place at about three o'clock in the morning. The sound drove my parents crazy because their bedroom looked out on the roof of the garage. It usually was followed by the slamming down of windows and a stream of curses from my father that the cats could not understand.

"I think that we as humans can all learn from Toots, Amanda. It is okay to be territorial and preserve what you believe in; however, at the end of the day you should also be able to welcome your neighbours into your territory and share and be enriched by their company.

"After all — this land was made for you and me."

21
Lost and Found

"Show me the way to go home,
I'm tired and I want to go to bed . . .
— From the lyrics by Irving King

"TC, I saw you and your friend Mike standing on top of a pile of mud, sticks and tree branches. It looked like a pond in the background. What were you and Mike doing?"

"We were standing on a beaver dam, Amanda, and we were lost. Let me tell you about that memory."

TC settled into his rocking chair. His pipe remained in the rack, unused. He closed his eyes and thought back in time.

"Mike and I were spending the summer together at our Amethyst Harbour cottage. The cottage was located on North Bay. There was a creek that flowed between our property and the neighbour's property. Some of the old timers in the area called it Beaver Creek, but we didn't know why. The creek provided Mike and I with an endless source of entertainment. We could build a dam where the creek entered the bay, we could catch tadpoles, we could have toy boat races in the flowing water, and there was a small pond upstream where we could fish for brook trout."

"You mentioned tadpoles, TC. What are they?"

TC's cough had returned. Amanda waited several minutes for the coughing episode to end. Then TC resumed the narrative.

"A tadpole or a pollywog is a baby frog that swims around in the water. They have a large flattened tail which allows them to wiggle or swim and they have no arms or legs. As they grow older the legs develop first, followed by the arms. Then the tail becomes shorter, the eyes get larger and the small mouth at the front of the head grows wider. The little frog then starts to breathe air and emerge from the water. It is really quite wonderful how different animals evolve."

"Is a frog really an animal? It sure doesn't look like one."

"It is a class of animal, Amanda. It is related to snakes, turtles and crocodiles. Oddly enough it is very much like a bird.

"Mike and I used to have races with the baby frogs. We would draw a circle in the sand and then we would each put a frog in the middle of the circle. The first frog to hop out of the circle won the race. Sometimes we would get our frogs mixed up because they all look alike. We also had to keep Toots away from our game because she liked to chase and catch the frogs."

"So what do frogs have to do with beaver dams?"

"I'm sorry, Amanda. I sometimes get my memories mixed up. But actually tadpoles and frogs are pretty interesting. Now, let me get back to my story.

"One day Mike and I decided that we would explore the creek and find out where it began. It was morning, so we packed up some peanut butter sandwiches and a couple of bottles of pop for lunch. There was no canned pop in those days. It all came in bottles. Mike decided to take along a compass so that we would not get lost. That compass was to become a big source of disagreement between Mike and me.

"We packed our knapsack and started off on the exploration trip. As usual Toots decided to follow along. She thought that there might be some good hunting on the way. There was a fisherman's path on one side of the creek, which made the first part of our trip pretty easy. But soon the creek became smaller and shallower with no pools for the brook trout. The path disappeared and only an animal track remained. Mike and I made our way upstream for several kilometres and eventually found the beaver dam. No wonder that the locals called it Beaver Creek.

"The creek emerged into an area clear of small trees and brush, with only a few large birch and poplar trees remaining. A forest of small stumps with neatly chewed spear-like ends guarded the pond. The dam stretched in an arc around more than half the perimeter. There was a pile of branches and twigs, all covered in mud near the edge of the pond. It was the beaver's home, a lodge. There was no entrance visible. It was underwater so that no intruder could get in.

"Mike and I scanned the water looking for telltale ripples or the exposed head of a beaver. There were none visible. Beavers are nocturnal animals that work at night and sleep by day. We sat down at the edge of the dam, opened the knapsack and ate our lunch. Toots took off after a chipmunk. It was an endless game of hide-and-seek. With no beavers in sight and the source of the creek discovered, Mike and I decided to head back to the cottage.

"Rather than returning by way of the creek we decided to head for a road to the cottage. It was called the North Bay Road. After a discussion we decided that since we had come from North Bay that we would use Mike's compass to find our way home. The trouble was that Mike's older brother had given him the compass and had not explained how to use it. We decided that since we knew the compass needle pointed north, then all we had to do was to walk in that direction and we would reach the North Bay road. We started out quite confident, the compass reading was quite simple and we would be home in time for supper. An hour later we were not sure and two hours later we knew that we were lost.

"I was an avid reader and a collector of Hardy Boy books. In one story Frank Hardy was lost and found his way home by checking the growth of moss on trees. According to the story, since the sun shines on the south side of the tree, the moss will grow on the shaded or north side of the tree. The problem was that there were so many trees, that there was no sun and the moss grew on all sides of the tree. Finally we found an open area and there was some moss on one side of several trees.

"I assured Mike that now we knew which way was north, we could find our way home. Mike in the meantime was shaking his head. His compass had merely confirmed my tree theory. We were still lost. We should have just followed the creek back."

"What happened to you and Mike next, TC? This is a pretty long story."

"Well Toots came to our rescue. It had been a long day and she had not caught any mice. She was hungry and decided to head for home. Cats have a remarkable homing instinct, which she had demonstrated on numerous occasions. Toots knew exactly where we were. Mike and I had actually been walking in a circle and the creek was not far away. We decided to follow Toots. We were back at the creek in about thirty minutes and from there it was an easy return to the cottage.

"Toots had found our way home."

22
The Piano

"Life is like a piano . . .
what you get out of it depends on how you play it."
— Anon

"I think that you are playing a joke on me, TC. When I looked through the keyhole I saw Toots playing the piano. The piano looked just like the one in our living room. Cats cannot play the piano. I know that."

Amanda had looked through the keyhole and did in fact see Toots playing the piano. Except there was never any sound when she looked through the keyhole, so she did not know what Toots was playing.

"Sit on the step, Amanda, and I will explain what you saw."

TC had a bad coughing spell. He was not getting any better and his cough was getting worse. He was no longer smoking his pipe. In a few minutes he had recovered.

"First of all, Amanda, cats cannot play the piano like a musician, but they can play at the piano. Toots was playing at the piano. Cats are very intelligent animals and they also have a sense of hearing far greater than you and I. Toots was a curious cat and she had watched my mother sitting on the piano bench and playing the piano by hitting the keys. She had thought to herself, *I can do that*. So she did. The trouble was that she tried it out for the first time in the middle of the night and woke the whole family up. It was 3:00 a.m. and my grandmother got up and went downstairs to find out what was going on. But there was no one at the piano and no one in the living room. Toots had fled the scene. It was a mystery.

"And then it happened again. Grandma was on the scene much quicker this time and she saw Toots disappearing down to her basket in the basement. The problem was quickly solved by closing the cover on the keyboard so that the piano could not be played."

"Then what happened?"

"Let me tell you a little bit about the piano first, Amanda. It has played a very important part in the history of our family. The piano is an upright Poole piano manufactured in Boston, Massachusetts. My mother was given the piano when she was in her teens and it has travelled with our family ever since. Remember the Pugmcishin Store that I told you about, Amanda. The piano box that we used for the store was the same box that my parents used to transport the piano from place to place. It was a beautiful piano, made out of rosewood with ivory capped keys. My mother gave the piano to me and I gave the piano to your mother. The piano is now more than one hundred years old and I hope that it stays in the family.

"When I was growing up the piano played a very big part in our lives. There was no television and radio was just in its infancy. We entertained ourselves by playing and singing songs around the piano. Both my mother and my sister played so there was no shortage of pianists. We loved music. I never learned to play but I do love to sing. Toots used to sit and watch and listen whenever the piano was being played.

"After we discovered Toots' interest in the piano we would let her sit on the bench so her paws could reach the piano keys. She would watch which keys were making the sound. My sister would sound a note on one key and then Toots learned to pick out the same key and sound the same note. It was quite amazing. If my sister sounded a key one octave higher, Toots would know which key to press.

"What is an octave, TC?"

TC slowly got up from his chair and took Amanda over to the piano in the living room.

"Okay, Amanda, press down on any white key."

Amanda sounded a white key on the left side of the keyboard.

"Now count over seven keys and sound the key."

Amanda counted and then pressed another white key.

"Okay, what did it sound like?"

"Well it sounded the same but it was different. It was higher."

"That is correct, Amanda. There are twelve notes in an octave with seven white keys and five black keys and as you move from left to right on the keyboard, each octave sounds higher. It is called the pitch or frequency of sound.

"As I said before, cats have excellent hearing. It is much better than humans, particularly for high pitch sounds."

"Do you think that a cat could ever learn to play music?"

"No, Amanda, our brains are not the same. Humans can create, remember and play beautiful piano music, but a cat can only imitate."

23
Flower's Children

*"A friend is one of the nicest things
to have and one of the nicest things to see."*
— Anon

"TC, I looked through the keyhole and I saw Toots carrying a baby skunk by the scruff of the neck. She was coming out of the door to your basement and there was a mother skunk waiting for her. What was going on?"

"Oh that was Toots carrying one of Flower's children. Flower was the name of the mother skunk and she was a good friend of Toots."

"Do you mean that cats and skunks can be friends?" Amanda asked.

"Of course," TC replied. "They are very similar in many ways, but they come from different families. They have no fear of each other and can actually live together. I don't know when Toots met Flower, but they had been friends for a long time."

"Why did you call the skunk Flower?"

The Keyhole

"Well, Amanda, when I was growing up there was a movie about a deer named Bambi and his best friends were Thumper the loveable rabbit, Flower the bashful skunk and his girlfriend Faline. It was a great story and when I saw that Toots and the skunk were friends, I decided to name the skunk Flower.

"My parents did not like skunks. They were always getting into the garbage and they dug up our lawn looking for white grubs. The dogs in our neighbourhood never learned. They would chase the skunks and the skunks would turn and spray them in defense. The scent from the encounter would last for several days. When Toots met a skunk they would each go through the usual smelling and greeting routine and then continue on their way. This usually happened in the evening or at night because skunks are nocturnal.

"One of the things that both cats and skunks share is a love of cat food. Flower had a very good sense of smell and she knew when Toots had left some cat food in her basement bowl. It was evening. Toots had left to visit a boyfriend at the end of the street. Usually our outside basement door was locked, but on some occasions the door was left open. On this particular evening the door was open. Flower came by, saw the open door and decided to check out the bowl in the basement. She could smell cat food and it was her favourite. It was fish.

"The trouble was that Flower had recently produced a litter of three kits or baby skunks. The kits followed Flower around wherever she went looking for food. Flower had no difficulty descending the stairs to the basement, but the kits followed and since they were not familiar with stairs, they just tumbled to the bottom. Flower headed for Toots' bowl and started to eat the cat food. The kits decided to join in.

"At about the same time my grandmother decided to get some pickles from the basement pantry and discovered Flower and the kits helping themselves to the cat food. Grandma did not scream. Grandma was not stupid. She knew that any hostile encounter with a skunk would result in a spray that would linger in the house for weeks."

Amanda was curious. "What did she do?"

"Well Grandma knew that skunks did not like mothballs, so she went back upstairs, found a box of mothballs and then scattered them around Toots' bowl and basket. Flower did not like mothballs and since there was no more cat food, decided that it was a good time to leave. She headed up the stair and through the door to the outside.

"The only problem was that the kits could not climb up the stairs. They did not know how. Flower had not taught them to climb stairs.

"Grandma did not know what to do. She knew that skunk kits can spray from birth and she was not going to take any chances. She called on me to help her get rid of the skunks. I suggested putting a board on the steps so that they could walk out on the board. It was a great idea but Flower was still guarding the door and I was afraid of being sprayed. We were at an impasse.

"It was Toots who came to the rescue. She had returned from her date and saw Flower standing guard at the basement door. She went over and smelled Flower in greeting. I don't know how Flower and Toots communicated, but Toots immediately went down the basement stairs, grabbed one of the kits by the scruff of the neck and presented it to Flower.

"That is what you saw through the keyhole, Amanda."

"What about the other two kits?" Amanda asked.

The Keyhole

TC resumed the story: "Toots repeated the rescue and all the kits were reunited with Flower. There was no exchange of thanks between Toots and Flower. The skunks slowly paraded off and Toots went down the basement to find her bowl of cat food empty."

"That was not a very good way for a friend to say *thank you*," Amanda commented.

24

The Kelvinator

"It's too easy to blame someone else."
— Anon

Amanda ran to the house looking for TC. He was on the front porch as usual.

"TC, when I looked through the keyhole today you were in the kitchen wiping up a puddle on the floor. Toots was also sitting in the kitchen watching you. What were you doing in that memory story?"

"Oh that was the time Toots was blamed for going to the bathroom in the kitchen instead of using her litter box in the basement. Sit down on the step, Amanda, and I will tell you the story."

Amanda sat down and waited as TC filled his pipe and settled back in his rocking chair. Regardless of a persistent cough, TC had fallen off the wagon and was smoking again.

"When I was a young boy we had an ice box to keep our food cool so that it would not spoil. The ice box was located in the back porch so that the ice man could come and replace the ice without entering the kitchen. Another reason that it was in the back porch was because the drain pan was always overflowing. When the ice melted inside the refrigerator it drained into a pan underneath. I was supposed to empty the pan every day but sometimes I forgot and it overflowed."

"What is an iceman, TC? It sounds like he was made out of ice."

TC laughed: "No he was not made out of ice, Amanda. He just delivered the ice to us in his ice truck. The blocks of ice were cut in the winter when the lake froze. When the ice became thick the cutters would then drill holes in the ice and use big saws to cut the ice into small blocks. Then they would take the blocks to an ice house and cover them with leftover sawdust from the lumber mills. The sawdust acted like insulation and kept the ice from melting.

"When the weather became warmer, we needed a refrigerator to keep our food fresh. The iceman would deliver the blocks of ice in his truck. He usually came twice a week and we would line up behind his truck waiting for him to wash off the sawdust and trim the ice. He would wipe off the sawdust and then use an ice pick to shape the ice so that it would fit inside the metal box at the top of the refrigerator. Then he would use metal tongs to grab hold of the block of ice so that he could carry it to the refrigerator.

"As soon as he left we would pick up the small pieces of ice that he had left and suck them. Toots was usually with us and we would give her a small piece of ice that she could lick."

"What does that have to do with the puddle on the kitchen floor?" Amanda asked.

"Don't be impatient, Amanda. I'm getting there."

TC's pipe had gone out. He struck a match to relight it.

"One day my father announced that he had just bought a newfangled appliance called a Kelvinator refrigerator. The icebox would be retired from duty in the back porch and the new refrigerator would find a home in the kitchen where there was an electrical outlet to plug it in. The entire family was very proud of this new appliance and we all stood around admiring the smooth rounded edges and its bright white finish. It even had a freezer and made little cubes of ice. Visitors to our home would be invited into the kitchen to see and admire the new Kelvinator. Even Toots was impressed because she quickly learned that the Kelvinator was a source of food. She was always there when the door was opened to see if there were any treats for her."

"Why was the refrigerator called a Kelvinator?"

"The people that manufactured the refrigerator were trying to think up a new name for this appliance and someone suggested that since a man by the name of Kelvin had discovered the coldest temperature at which nothing could get colder, then they should call the new appliance a Kelvinator. They hoped that people would think that nothing could get colder than a Kelvinator refrigerator and they would buy it."

"Was that true, TC?"

"Not really. I am sure that my parents did not know who Lord Kelvin was or what he had invented. It's called marketing. But let me continue with my story.

"About a month after the Kelvinator had arrived I came down from my bedroom for breakfast. I was always the first one up because I had to deliver newspapers in the morning, before I went to school. Toots was always in the kitchen waiting for a treat. I was quite surprised to find a puddle of water in the middle of the kitchen floor. It was yellow and it looked like urine. I assumed that Toots had gone to the bathroom and had not used her litter box. I scolded Toots, wiped up the puddle, had my breakfast and went off to deliver my newspapers. Toots did not get a treat that day.

"I didn't really think about the puddle or tell anyone that I had cleaned it up. Both my grandmother and my parents thought that Toots was getting old and should be put away, so I didn't tell them about the accident.

"About one week later the same thing happened. This time I was annoyed and I grabbed Toots and rubbed her nose in the puddle and said 'bad cat! Bad cat!'

"Toots ran to her basket in the basement and started to clean her face. This time my grandmother found me cleaning up and asked what I was doing. I had to explain that Toots had gone to the bathroom and left a puddle on the floor.

"My grandmother told me that when cats get old that they lose control and have accidents. She thought that it was probably time for Toots to be put away and told my parents."

"I guess that Toots was in big trouble," Amanda remarked. "Why didn't you just take her to the vet and he could give her a pill or something."

"There were no vets at that time and there were no pills for cats that made puddles," TC replied. "Yes Toots was in big trouble. My parents announced that the next time there was a puddle, Toots would have to go. Well, Amanda, there was another puddle and again I rubbed Toots' nose in the urine and scolded her. I didn't tell anyone about the accident.

"Then it happened again, but this time was different because Toots was in the middle of the floor licking up the puddle. I thought that this was strange and I put my finger in the puddle and tasted it. It was just like water. I tried it again. It was water!

"I took a closer look at the floor and I could see a faint trickle of water coming from the Kelvinator. The new refrigerator was leaking."

"So it wasn't Toots that made the puddle!" Amanda exclaimed.

"Toots was not to blame, Amanda. In your life you be very careful who you blame, because you might be wrong. I had to apologize. All I could say was, 'I'm sorry Toots, and I love you.'

"I think she understood me. She just raised her tail and purred."

25
Trapped

"When you can't find a way out, it's best to find a way further in."
— Abdelrahman Ashraf Abuzied

"TC! I was looking through the keyhole and there was a fireman climbing down a ladder by the side of your house. He was carrying a cat with in one arm and holding onto the ladder with the other arm. What was going on?"

TC settled back in his rocking chair and started to cough. He recovered and then put his unlit pipe back in the pipe rack. He was ready for another memory story.

"Well, as you know my mother always called the fire department when there was a problem. It was a good thing that the fire station was only a short distance away, because they were called quite often and usually Toots had something to do with the call. This was no exception.

"When the house was originally constructed it had no insulation in the walls and no insulation in the ceiling. My dad had decided that it was costing too much money to heat the house in the winter and the upstairs was always very hot in the summer. Since sawdust and wood chips were readily available in Fort William, he decided to use these materials to insulate the walls and the second floor ceiling.

"Because of the mess during construction our family decided to move down to the cottage at Amethyst for two weeks leaving only dad and Toots as supervisors.

"Dad had selected an insulation company and they began the slow and expensive process of opening up the top of the walls and pouring sawdust in the cavities. When they got to the ceiling they used wood chips and easily spread the chips between the rafters in the attic."

"Why didn't they use fiberglass or plastic foam?" Amanda asked.

"Those products are available now, Amanda, but they had not been invented when I was a boy. Since dad was away at work during the day, he left Toots in charge. Toots was very interested in what was going on. She knew from experience that there were mice in the walls and also in the attic. She had heard the mice and smelled them. She was hoping that a mouse would be discovered and that she would be there to catch it. My parents regularly put some traps in the attic to catch the mice.

"In order to insulate the second floor ceiling the contractor had to put up a ladder to an access hatch in the ceiling. Bags of wood chips could then be pushed through the access hatch into the attic. The bags would then be emptied and the chips spread between the ceiling joists. Toots would sit in the hall for hours and watch this operation with occasional trips to the litter box for a drink of water.

The Keyhole

"It was after the attic work had been completed, the hatch had been closed and the contractor had departed, that Toots went missing. My dad was not concerned. Toots often wandered off on one of her hunting trips. She always came back for breakfast.

"But she did not appear for the morning meal and she was not at home when dad returned from the office at the end of the day. Dad made a tour to see if any of our neighbours had seen the missing cat. There had been no sightings. Three more days passed. There was still no sign of Toots. This was getting serious. Dad decided that since the insulation work was now complete that the family should return home, a few days early, from our cottage at Amethyst and assist in the search for Toots.

"When I arrived home, I immediately made a tour of Toot's favourite hiding spots. There was no sign of Toots. I checked out some of the neighbours who occasionally gave her a free meal, but still no luck. My mother phoned the pound to see if she had strayed or been picked up. No luck. There were no reports of a street car or automobile accident involving a cat.

"One week had now passed since Toots went missing. The first tip came from our neighbour Alf Hannigan. Although he was deaf in one ear, Alf said that he had been walking his dog and he had heard a mewing sound coming from our house. It seemed to be up near the roof.

"I went out to check. Alf was right I could also hear a mewing sound. It was definitely coming from the soffit of the roof. I ran to tell my mother who came outside. She looked up and heard the mewing sound as well."

"What's a soffit?"

Amanda and TC were sitting on the front porch. TC pointed up to the roof.

"Do you see how the roof overhangs the wall of the house? The soffit is that flat underside of the overhang. There is enough empty space above the soffit for a cat. The problem was that the soffit was too high. It could not be reached. As usual my mother called the fire department.

"That is what you saw when you looked through the keyhole, Amanda. Toots was inside the soffit. The firemen had to climb up on their ladder and locate where the sound was coming from. The mewing continued. Fortunately there were some ventilation holes in the soffit. The sound seemed to come from one hole. The fireman made the hole bigger using a keyhole saw, and sure enough Toots poked her head out. The fireman enlarged the hole. Toots was so thin that the fireman could easily pull her through the hole. She was covered with small pieces of wood chips and she was so weak that she could hardly stand. I brought her a bowl of cool water and she emptied it. She started to groom herself. That was a good sign. Toots was safe and we thanked the fireman for the rescue. The fireman was not pleased."

"Our job is to put out fires and not to rescue cats that get into trouble," he replied. "We don't want any more calls about your cat."

Little did the fireman know that there would be many more phone calls for his assistance.

"Well that's a good story, TC, but I do not understand. How did Toots get stranded in the soffit?"

"Toots knew how to climb a ladder," TC replied.

"Most cats can climb ladders. I think that just before the workmen closed up the hatch, Toots decided to climb the ladder and check out the attic for herself. She went up there looking for mice and when the hatch was closed, Toots was trapped. The workmen did not know that she was in the attic. Nobody knew that she was there.

"The attic gets very hot in the summer and so Toots went to one of the ventilation holes in the soffit to cool off and to get some fresh air. My dad could not hear her mewing from inside the house. It was just lucky that our neighbour Alf heard the sound from the outside, when he was out walking his dog. If Toots had chosen the wrong side of the house for some fresh air, no one would have heard her. She would have died up there."

"Toots was trapped," Amanda remarked.

"I guess it was a new experience for her. When you can't find a way out, it's best to find a further way in."

26
Cat Play

"When I play with my cat, she knows whether she is not amusing herself with me more than I with her."
– Montaigne

"TC, I looked through the keyhole and you were sitting on a chair near Toots' basket, watching the kittens. They seemed to be having a good time playing together."

As usual TC was sitting on his rocking chair on the front porch. His cough had persisted and TC was trying to observe the 'No Smoking' ban imposed on him by Amanda's mother.

"Sit down, Amanda, and I will tell you what I know about kittens and play. I call it the joy of kittenhood. I really think that it is the best time in the life of a cat. I always enjoyed watching the kittens play with each other and when they grew older, I enjoyed playing with them.

"Most mammals play when they are youngsters and some continue even when they are grown up. Some birds play, but I have never known fish or cold-blooded frogs or snakes to play. The most playful species are dolphins, apes, monkeys and most carnivores."

"What are carnivores, TC?"

"A carnivore is a bird or a mammal that eats other animals that feed on grasses and plants. Sometimes they eat other carnivores. Carnivores include all of the cat family such as lions or tigers and raptors such as crows or owls. Usually carnivores are highly intelligent."

"Why do kittens play with each other?"

"Kittens learn by playing. It teaches them to get along with each other, how to survive, how to hunt and how to keep physically fit. You know, Amanda, I often think that we as human beings would be much better off if we had spent more time playing in our childhood.

"It takes about three weeks before a kitten is interested in playing. By that time they can see and they are not busy feeding. It is mostly rough and tumble play. By the fourth week they have learned how to wrestle with each other, clasping with their front paws and kicking with their rear legs. By the fifth week they have learned to pounce on each other. This is a skill that will be used in their adult life to catch mice. Swatting and scooping come next, in preparation for hunting birds and fish. It is usually these traits that are used when cats play with humans.

"They will mouse pounce on a trailing piece of string or the twitching end of Toots' tail. They will bird swat at a dangling piece of ribbon and fish scoop a rolling ball of string. It is all about learning and practicing by playing.

"As the kittens grow older there is less play and by the time they become adults, playing is rare. The love of play is never completely lost. Even old cats can be encouraged to chase a rolling ball or swat at an imaginary bird. I always felt sorry for kittens that grow up alone and do not have the stimulation of playing with brothers and sisters.

"With Toots in charge, there was never any danger of that happening in our home. We had an endless supply of kittens and I had continuous entertainment."

As TC told this story, Amanda had kept her hands on her ears.

"Why do you have your hands on your ears, Amanda? Are you not interested in this memory?"

"Oh, I can hear you all right, TC. I am just fixing my ears."

"What do you mean?"

Amanda blushed and removed her hands from her ears. Her hair was braided behind her ears with the braids out front. One ear remained tight to her head and the other popped out. Amanda pushed it toward her head, but it popped out again. She was embarrassed.

"TC, I think that my ears stick out too much and I was just trying to fix them with this tape."

Amanda removed two pieces of grey duct tape from behind her ears that she had folded over and were sticky on both sides.

"This tape is not working very well. I will have to try something else."

TC rubbed his forehead, searching for the right words to reply: "Amanda, your ears are quite normal. When you are young, your head and your ears are about the same size that they will be when you are an adult. The rest of your body has to catch up. When I was your age I thought that my head was too big and I worried about it. I checked in the mirror each day to see if it had grown any bigger. I thought that I looked like a freak."

"Well some of the boys at school tease me and call me Dumbo, just like the cartoon elephant with big ears."

TC laughed: "Well, at least Dumbo could fly. But seriously, Amanda, we all have hang-ups about ourselves and things that we don't like about our appearance. You have to learn to believe in yourself and who you are. Nobody will pay any attention to your ears. They are more interested in you as a person."

"Well, thanks for your advice, TC," Amanda replied. Then there was a pause.

"Maybe I should wear my braids in front of my ears?"

TC closed his eyes and shook his head. His good advice had apparently fallen on deaf ears.

27

Stuck

"TC, when I looked through the keyhole there was a fire truck in front of your house and one of the firemen was in a ditch looking into a drainage pipe. What was that all about?"

"I am a little bit embarrassed about that memory, Amanda. I got into a great deal of trouble that day. It is a memory that I would rather forget."

"Tell me about it, TC! Please tell me about it! Was Toots involved in this memory?"

"Well as you know, Amanda, Toots is usually involved in my memories. Toots was a young cat when this story happened.

"Our street was not paved and there were ditches on either side of the road for drainage. My father did not like the appearance of the ditch and had installed a corrugated steel culvert pipe in front of our house and had it covered over with soil and planted with grass.

"One of the games that my friends and I played was our version of cricket. We called it can- the-can. Instead of a wicket we used six tin cans with three at the bottom, two in the middle and one on top. A baseball bat was used instead of a paddle bat and a tennis ball substituted for a cricket ball. We had our own set of rules because there were never enough players to make up a team."

"Do you throw the ball overarm like hardball or underarm like softball?" Amanda asked.

"Originally a cricket ball was thrown underarm and rolled along the ground. That is why they still use the term bowler. Now the ball is thrown overarm but it must hit the ground before hitting the wicket. "It was a Friday and school was out for the weekend. My friends and I decided to have a game of can-the-can. Toots had joined us. She had discovered a family of mice that lived in the ditch. They had a nest near the entrance to our culvert. Toots lay on the grass above the entrance in fine hunting form and waited for a victim, while we played can-the-can.

"We were not paying any attention to Toots. Our game was just getting underway when she saw a mouse and pounced. The mouse got away and ran toward the culvert pipe. Toots followed and the mouse and Toots both disappeared into the end of the pipe.

"I had been sitting on the edge of the ditch waiting for my turn to bat and saw what had happened. When Toots did not reappear, I became worried and went over to the entrance of the culvert pipe, kneeled down and looked inside. I could see two eyes gleaming in the dark. Toots was about six feet away waiting for the mouse to reappear. I called, but she would not come out. Cats will wait forever if they think there is a mouse to catch.

"It was my turn to bat, so I left Toots in the culvert pipe and continued our game of can-the-can. After about an hour of play it was time for supper. I checked the culvert and Toots was still inside. I called, but she would still not come out. I decided to crawl into the culvert pipe and rescue Toots. That was a big mistake."

"What do you mean, TC?"

"The culvert was just big enough that I could lie down on my stomach with arms stretched out. Using my hands to grip the sides of the pipe, I could pull myself forward. I could almost reach Toots, but she turned and ran out the other end of the pipe.

"Then I discovered that although I could move forward, I could not back out. I was stuck and I called to my friends for help. My friend Mike ran to our house to tell my mother. She went to the ditch, took one look at my feet sticking out the end and decided to phone the fire department. She always called the fire department in an emergency. A fire truck appeared within minutes with sirens blaring and lights flashing. A group of neighbours gathered to watch the latest action.

"Both firemen had been involved in the previous rescue of Toots from the soffit and Toots and I in the birch tree. They were not pleased with this latest call and informed my mother that they would have to charge her for these unnecessary trips and false alarms."

"Did the firemen get you out of the culvert pipe?"

"They were quite clever, Amanda. The firemen had some rope in the truck and they tied it around my ankles. In minutes they had pulled me out of the pipe. I ended up with a few bruises and scrapes.

"Toots had been watching the rescue. While I was sitting at the side of the ditch recovering, she rubbed past my legs with tail erect and then stopped and licked the rope burns on my ankles. I guess it was her way of saying, 'I'm sorry.'"

28
Smokey

"TC! TC! I saw Toots running from a grass fire and she was holding a kitten by the scruff of the neck. I think that you were trying to put out the fire and were hitting at it with a sack. There were three other boys helping you. There was smoke everywhere. What was going on?"

TC pulled a match out his pocket and showed it to Amanda.

"Don't play with these, Amanda. That simple little stick can cause a lot of damage. Always treat it with respect. I am afraid that I learned that little lesson the hard way. Let me tell you about the grass fire and how Toots adopted a kitten.

"Remember my story about the secret hideout behind Vickers Park and about the abandoned subdivision with ditches and fields. That is where this memory takes place. It was a weekend in spring. The snow had disappeared from the fields with the long brown grass from the previous year pressed close to the ground. The soil was still soggy from the winter melt but the grass was dry.

"My blood brothers and I were having a meeting at our hideout. The ditch was a little wet, so we had decided to dry things out with a fire. We had trouble starting the fire because the twigs and kindling were still wet from the winter snow. Some birch bark peeled from one of the park trees solved the problem.

"Toots had just produced a litter of kittens and decided to take some time off for mousing in the fields. When we went to our hideout we found that it had been taken over by a family of cats. There was no sign of the mother. She had probably been run over or attacked by coyotes. Five malnourished little kittens remained. Four were dead and one had survived.

"Toots immediately took charge. She cuddled up to the surviving kitten and licked it clean. The kitten found a nipple and sucked. Toots still had milk. In the meantime I found a shovel and buried the dead kittens. Mike was busy with the fire while Jim and Ron cleaned up.

"I have no idea how the grass fire started, but it was windy and a random spark must have ignited some grass close to our hideout. Grass fires are tricky. They can sort of smolder and spread unnoticed. Then the fire will flare up and spread very quickly producing a great deal of smoke.

"We had some sacks in the hideout that we could use to beat out the flames. With the four of us working we thought the fire was under control, but it sprang up in three more locations, ignited by airborne hot ash. The wind was our enemy. The fire was out of control. We could hear the fire trucks coming. Someone had seen the smoke and alerted the fire department. We decided to flee the scene. Toots was ahead of us carrying the surviving kitten by the scruff of the neck."

"That is what I saw through the keyhole," Amanda joined in. "Then what happened, TC?"

"Well, we watched what was going on from the park. The fire trucks arrived, but there were no fire hydrants to supply water. The fields were still too wet to support the pumper truck. It would have got stuck. The firemen had to backpack fifty-pound water canisters over uneven ground to chase the fire. The ditches did not stop the rampage. The wind merely carried hot embers to the neighbouring fields. It took several hours to get the fire under control.

"While we were sitting in the park watching the firemen at work, a police officer approached us. He said that there were reports of some small boys playing in the fields before the fire started. He then asked if we were the boys and if we had started the fire.

"We all looked at each other and remembered our blood brother oath. We did not tell lies, but we stuck together. I stood up for the group and admitted that it was us.

"The police officer announced that he could take us all down to the police station and charge us with arson. It was also very expensive to have the fire department out fighting a grass fire. We could be fined for the cost involved.

"I pleaded that the fire had not been deliberate and that when it started we had tried our best to put it out. The wind had made that impossible. The police officer relented and left us with a warning that if this ever happened again that we would all go to jail."

"What happened to the kitten, TC?"

"Well, that part of the memory had a happy ending. Toots adopted the kitten as one of her own and I named the kitten Smokey. I never told my mother about the fire and she never counted the kittens. Smokey was accepted by our family and eventually found a very nice home on a farm."

29
Pinocchio

*"A lie keeps growing and growing
until it's as plain as the nose on your face."*
— The Blue Fairy in the Pinocchio Movie

"TC, I saw Toots sitting looking at a bowl with some fish in it. What was happening in that memory?"

TC was not out on the front porch. He was inside the house, sitting in his rocking chair and was all bundled up in a blanket. He was coughing and did not look well.

"Are you okay?" asked Amanda.

"Give me a minute. Let me remember. Oh yes.

"I had two goldfish called Goldie and Whitey that I kept in my bedroom. They were in a glass bowl and I was responsible for feeding them and changing the water. Toots would spend hours watching the fish swimming around. Occasionally she would get thirsty and take a drink from the bowl. She had tried to put her paw in the bowl to catch the fish but was quickly discouraged. It was awkward and she did not like getting her feet wet.

"One day I found Whitey floating belly up in the top of the bowl. I think that Whitey died of natural causes. Toots did not seem interested. A few weeks later our maid Lena reported to my mother that Goldie was gone. The bowl was now empty. Of course Toots was blamed.

"My mother quickly announced that there would be no more fish in the house. She ordered me to empty out the water and to put the bowl away. She also announced that she was sick and tired of Toots getting into trouble. It was just one thing after another. Toots would have to go!

"Well, I burst into tears with this announcement and admitted that Toots had not killed Goldie, but that I had flushed Goldie down the toilet when I was changing the water. I did not want to admit that I had killed Goldie but I also knew that Toots was not to blame."

"Did your nose grow longer like Pinocchio's nose?" Amanda asked. "Well, it should have grown longer. I had not told a lie, Amanda, but I had also not told the truth about Goldie. I had let others incriminate my own innocent cat without saying anything. It was worse than telling a lie."

Amanda had her notebook out and was busy writing. "Why are you taking notes, Amanda?"

"I keep a diary and each night I write down the events of the day. When I look through the keyhole and you tell me one of your stories about Toots. I write it down. Someday I intend to be a famous writer and I will use some of this material for a book."

TC smiled: "In that case I will have to be very careful about what I say, but I really like the idea of keeping a diary and your plan to become a journalist. It is important to set your life goals early and work toward them."

"All of my English marks are in the high nineties, TC, and I may be promoted to an Advancement Class."

"That would be great, Amanda. I skipped Grade Four when I was going to school."

"I think I may be skipping two grades," Amanda replied.

30
Unwanted Guests

"A guest is like rain: when he lingers on,
he becomes a nuisance."
— Yiddish Proverb

"I saw Toots in your living room, staring at the fireplace. What was she looking at, TC?"

"Well, Amanda, we all wondered about that as well. It was a mystery. It was early September and we had returned from the cottage. Toots was happy to be home and made her usual rounds to check out her territory. The fireplace was only used in the fall and winter months. The damper was kept closed when there was no fire. Toots stopped at the fireplace during her inspection of the house and stared at the opening. In the summer we kept some birch logs in the fireplace, ready to be lit. Toots went over to the logs and looked up the flue. With the damper closed there was nothing to see. Then she sat down, stared straight ahead and waited. After ten or fifteen minutes she got up and went about her business. This little scene was repeated day after day.

"With fall approaching my grandmother decided that the fireplace needed to be cleaned. We usually started burning wood in October. She pulled out the decorative birch logs and carefully wrapped them up for use next summer. Next she kneeled down and shoveled out some leftover ashes onto a piece of newspaper. She pushed on the damper. It wouldn't open. She tried to wiggle it up and down. Some dried grass and straw fell down. She pushed the damper harder. There was an unfamiliar sound coming from the fireplace. It was something between a squeak and a chirp. Toots had been watching Grandma. She walked over to the fireplace and looked up to see a small white face punctuated with a black nose, two black eyes and a grey head. Three more similar heads appeared. Grandma couldn't see them and gave the damper one final push.

"Three baby raccoons fell to the floor of the fireplace along with the sooty remains of their nest, leftover food and waste. It was a real mess."

"What happened to the kits next?"

"Well Grandma was upset and screamed, but she had the presence of mind to open the front door. Then she ran to get a broom. The kits or baby raccoons took off in all directions scattering the debris, soot and ashes all over the living room rug. Toots chased one of the kits, caught it and carried it outside by the scruff of the neck. For some unknown reason, the mother raccoon after escaping up the flue, had climbed down from the roof and was waiting at the front door. She grabbed the kit from Toots and then carried it by the scruff of the neck back up the TV aerial, which she used as a ladder, crossed the roof and dropped the kit back down the chimney flue. We were back were we started with the three kits inside the house and momma waiting outside.

The Keyhole

"In the meantime I had heard Grandma's screams from inside the house and saw what was happening on the roof. I grabbed a small board, climbed the aerial and covered the chimney flue with the board. In the meantime Grandma and Toots were inside the house rounding up the baby raccoons.

"When Toots caught and carried the second kit outside, the mother raccoon just repeated her climb up the aerial and found the board covering the flue. Raccoons are very intelligent and can use their hands like a human. She easily removed the board and dropped the second kit down the flue. I am sure this would have made a great movie for everyone's amusement, but Grandma and I did not think it was very funny.

"When I saw the raccoon flip the board off the flue, I ran to the backyard and found some chicken mesh and some wire. I climbed up on the roof a second time and capped the flue tightly with the mesh and wire. That worked; the mother raccoon gave up on the flue and then ran and deposited each of the kits in our hedge."

"Do raccoons use chimney flues for their nests very often, TC?"

"As a matter of fact they do," TC replied.

"As far as the mother raccoon is concerned, a flue looks like a hollow log. It is also safe and up high. The space above the damper is a good place to build a nest and it is nice and dry. Raccoons are very misunderstood in our society. They think that we are excellent neighbours. They don't know that our delicious vegetable gardens, our overflowing garbage pails and our full bird feeders are not just for them. And when these clever critters take advantage of our hospitality, they get into trouble."

31
Just Friends

"Before a cat will condescend,
To treat you as a trusted friend,
Some little token of esteem,
Is needed, like a dish of cream."
— T. S. Eliot

Amanda looked through the keyhole and saw TC fast asleep with Toots curled up beside him, with her head on TC's shoulder. Amanda thought that she would ask TC about cat love and friendship. She headed for the house and found TC on the front verandah. She immediately described what she had seen through the keyhole.

"I was wondering, TC. I think that you loved Toots, but did Toots love you? Is that why she came home from Amethyst Harbour, or was it because she knew that she would be fed and have a nice warm place to stay and raise her kittens?"

TC was silent for a minute thinking of a good way to answer Amanda's question. He closed his eyes.

The Keyhole

"Amanda, you come up with the strangest questions. That is a really tough one for me to answer. The word love has many different meanings and interpretations. For instance you might say that you love your mother, but you also say that you love chocolate milk. You love your best friend Betty, but you also love the new dress that she is wearing. When you grow older you may find romantic love with a young man. If you marry, at your wedding ceremony you will vow *to love and to cherish until death do us part*.

"I think that we get the words love and like mixed up. I think that you probably love your mother, but you like chocolate milk. You may love Betty, but you like her new dress.

"I think that cats and humans show their feelings for each other in different ways. If I arrive home and open the door, a dog will run toward me and bark a greeting, with tail wagging. A cat will look up and ignore me. A few minutes later, the cat will get up, walk toward me with tail erect and brush past my leg marking her scent and accepting me into her territory, not my territory. That is not love.

"You saw Toots asleep and curled up beside me. Was she there because she loved me or was she there because it was a nice safe, warm and comfortable place to be?

"When I stroke her back, she purrs. Is that because she loves me, or is it because she just enjoys the attention?

"So in answer to your question, Amanda, I do not think that there was any love between us. I think that Toots was my friend and that I was just a friend of Toots."

"I have another question for you, TC. It's about friends. I have just been offered a promotion from my Grade Five class to advancement class in Grade Seven. I'm really excited about learning new things in Grade Seven, because I was getting bored in Grade Five. The trouble is that the class is in another school and I will lose all of my friends at the old school. What do you think I should do?"

"Well this is a great learning opportunity for you, Amanda, and you shouldn't worry about losing your old friends. You will meet many interesting students and make new friends. If your old friends are true friends, they will stick with you no matter where you are. In the end you will have more friends than you have now and many of these friends will be with you for the rest of your life."

Amanda gave TC a hug.

"Thanks, TC. I can hardly wait for the Grade Seven class to start."

32

Domino

"We'll be friends forever, won't we Pooh?" asked Piglet.
"Even longer," Pooh replied.
— A.A. Milne, Winnie-the-Pooh

"TC I saw you carrying a cage with an animal in it. What was that all about?" Amanda asked.

"That was an interesting memory," TC replied. "I will tell you all about it. It was the last day of school and my teacher, Miss Brownley, handed out the report cards. Everyone in the class had passed. We would all be going on to Grade Five. Then she asked for a volunteer, who would like to take care of Domino the hamster during the summer. Of course twenty hands were raised and Miss Brownley had a problem. She then decided that the student with the highest class average would get the hamster. I was the lucky person and I proudly took Domino home in its cage to show my parents. My mother was not pleased. My father was indifferent.

"'It's just one more animal that I have to care for. I am not going to have a dirty rodent in my house making a mess,' mother said. 'Take it back to school.'

"But taking it back to school was impossible. The school bus was no longer in service and Miss Brownley had quickly fled the premises leaving a note. 'See you in September — have a great summer!' written on the blackboard.

"Domino had a new home and as strange as it may seem, he had a new friend. It was Toots. Our class had decided that the hamster should have a name and so after much discussion we chose the name Domino because the hamster was black with white spots. I don't think that hamsters really care if they have a name or not. Domino never came when he was called. Miss Brownley had wisely decided to have only one hamster in the classroom. 'It controls the population,' she laughingly remarked. We didn't understand her humour.

"I used to go around the house with Domino perched on my shoulder. This really bugged my mother, but eventually she got used to it. Toots was fascinated. She had never seen a hamster before. It was bigger than a mouse but smaller than a rat. It was different. It didn't have a tail and its paws and nose were pink. It looked good enough to eat, but it didn't act like a mouse or a rat. Toots was undecided. Domino had spent most of his life at school and had no fear of humans. He also had no fear of cats. He had never seen a cat. He was just curious.

"On the very first day at our home I took Domino off my shoulder and put him down in front of Toots. Domino was not afraid. Why should he run? Having never seen a cat before, he walked slowly towards Toots and stuck his nose in her face. His bristly whiskers tickled Toots' nose and made her sneeze. Toots was confused. She batted Domino with her paw, claws pulled back so they wouldn't hurt. She only did this with her own kittens. Domino rolled over on his back thinking that this was some sort of a game. Toots thought that this was strange. He was acting just like a kitten. Domino had a new friend.

"Domino's cage was kept up on a counter in the kitchen. Toots would jump up on the counter and watch Domino when he was using his wheel. The 30 cm diameter wheel was an exercise device that most hamsters and rodents enjoy. It was made out of metal with a mesh running surface and mounted on a stand. Domino would run for hours and literally travel a great distance while exercising."

Amanda interrupted: "What did Domino eat? Did he like cat food?"

"Not really, he was more of a vegetarian, while Toots ate mostly meats and protein foods. Occasionally he would sneak a piece of cooked chicken or fish from Toots' bowl, but not often."

"Did you have to take Domino back to school at the end of the summer?" Amanda asked.

"The answer is no. The day before school started, Miss Brownley phoned and asked me if I would like to keep Domino. She had been given some rabbits and thought that they would provide a new learning experience for the class, including our sex education. I was overjoyed, but Miss Brownley said that I would have to get my parent's permission to keep Domino. I was smart and I knew from experience to ask my father first. He immediately said yes and promised that he would discuss it with my mother. That was when Domino became a permanent member of our family . . . until he disappeared."

"What do you mean he disappeared?" Amanda asked.

"Well, I woke up one morning and the cage was empty. I had forgotten to lock the door and Domino, who was a night person, decided to go exploring. We looked all over the house: under the beds, behind the furniture, in the cupboards and the closets. He was nowhere to be found. By the end of the day we gave up. I was crying and my mother was secretly happy. Toots was also upset. She just sat under the counter, where Domino had his cage, and stared at the wall.

"When I filled up her water bowl, Toots wouldn't drink and she had not touched her morning meal. It was all very unusual. She just kept staring at the wall.

"Finally I got down on my knees to see what she was staring at. I heard a noise. It was a squeak coming from inside the wall. Finally we had located Domino, but he was inside the wall. We could not get him out. I checked behind his cage on the counter and found a hole in the wall, which had once been used for a long forgotten electrical outlet. The outlet had been removed but the hole had never been patched. Domino had crawled through the hole and then fell to the bottom of the wall. There was no way for him to get out.

"My mother freaked out saying that Domino would die inside the wall and make an awful smell. She was ready to call the fire department. My father calmed her down and said that he would cut a hole in the bottom of the wall so that Domino could escape his self-made prison. In a few minutes the hole had been cut with a keyhole saw. Domino peaked out and then ran immediately to Toots. He was all covered with dirt and plaster. Toots began to clean him up by licking off the mess while Domino sat patiently between her paws. I never left the cage unlocked again.

"Domino had not used his wheel for days and his food bowl had not been touched. Domino was obviously sick and he spent most of the day sleeping. I didn't know what to do. I waited to see if he would improve. He did not get any better. Domino had lived with us for more than two years and in hamster time, he was very old.

"It was a Saturday morning when it happened. I opened the door of the cage and Domino came out slowly. He was looking for Toots and when Toots appeared he went and cuddled up in his favourite spot between her paws. Toots looked down and went through the usual routine of licking Domino's fur. Domino just closed his eyes and never opened them again. Domino had died.

"Toots continued to lick Domino and when she had finished, she grabbed him by the neck like a kitten and carried him back to his cage. Then she gave Domino a final goodbye lick and jumped from the counter."

33
Flushed

"Water, water, everywhere,
Nor any drop to drink."
— Rime of the Ancient Mariner, Samuel Taylor Coleridge

"TC, I just saw Toots drinking water out of your toilet. Was she allowed to do that?"

As usual TC was on the front verandah in his rocking chair and reading. He put down his newspaper and motioned for Amanda to sit down. He had been sick the previous week and there had been several visits from the doctor. Amanda's mother had been very concerned about TC's coughing and breathing problems.

"As a matter of fact, drinking out of the toilet was not allowed, but Toots never learned the rule and Toots never obeyed the rule. She just preferred toilet water rather than the water that we put in her bowl. My mother finally asked us to put the toilet lid down, but that request was often forgotten."

"Maybe it tasted better," Amanda suggested.

TC thought for a minute.

"Well I think that you may be correct, Amanda, because most cats prefer to have to have cool fresh water compared to warm, stale water that has been sitting in a bowl. Cats also do not like water that has been chlorinated, but all of our water came from a lake up in the mountains and was pure.

"Toots also liked to watch moving water. When we flushed the toilet she would sit and watch the water swirl around in a circle. Water running from a tap to fill a sink or a bathtub also was watched carefully. If we were at the cottage she would go down to the lake and watch the incoming waves and jump back at each new wave as it approached and then chase the wave as it receded. Swiftly flowing water in a stream was also an invitation for watching and drinking.

"I remember that one of Toots' kittens liked to sit in the basement laundry tub drinking water dripping from a constantly leaking tap. The trouble was she couldn't climb out of the tub and had to be rescued.

"I think that Toots' drinking and watching habits were all inherited from the cat family. This is what her ancestors used to do. Lions and tigers all loved to drink cool flowing water."

Amanda laughed: "You should have provided her with her own tap, TC, and taught her how to turn it on."

"Well don't laugh, Amanda. Cats may not know how to turn a tap but they do learn how to pull down on a lever and flush the toilet.

"You know, Amanda, there is reason to believe that water is more important for cats than it is for other animals. They drink more and they drink often. Cats have developed a highly efficient way of drinking that makes them quite different than other animals. A cat's tongue is long and flicks in and out very rapidly. The end of the tongue is curved like a spoon. The cat will flick it in and out creating a stream and then close its mouth and swallow.

"Try drinking from a bowl sometime and do it without getting your face wet. Cats can drink without getting their chin or whiskers wet. Dogs, horses and cows all drink by using their tongues, but they all do it more slowly and they all get their faces wet. Humans cannot drink with their tongue."

After listening to this memory, Amanda went to the kitchen, filled a bowl with water and tried to drink like a cat. TC was right. She ended up with a wet face and no water.

34
Sneezy

"There is no more intrepid an explorer than a kitten."
— Jules Champfleury

"TC, I just saw Toots carrying a really dirty kitten by the scruff of the neck. Was she hurting it?"

Amanda had found TC inside the house. It was late October and the cold front verandah had been replaced by the warmth and comfort of an indoor den and fireplace. TC added a log to the fire and pulled up his rocking chair. Smoking indoors was not allowed. TC's pipes remained in their rack on the front verandah. Amanda sat on a stool near the fire.

"No, Amanda. Toots was not hurting the kitten. That is the way that mother cats carry their young and it is really a sign of affection. However, you do not carry an older cat by the scruff of the neck because they are too heavy and it hurts them. Now, pull up a chair and I'll tell you the story about Sneezy and the coal storage room."

"The name sounds like one of the seven dwarfs," Amanda commented.

"You are right on, Amanda. As you know Toots usually had five kittens in a litter, but on this particular occasion she had seven babies. There were four males and three females. I had just seen the *Disney* movie about *Snow White and the Seven Dwarfs*, so we named the kittens after the dwarfs in spite of the fact that they were both male and female. There was Doc, Grumpy, Happy, Sleepy, Bashful, Dopey and Sneezy. Six of them had the same markings and looked alike, while the seventh one was completely black."

"How did you tell the other six apart?" Amanda asked.

"Well we started off by putting name tags on them, but after we got to know them, we changed their name tags to suit their personality.

"Sneezy was the easiest kitten to recognize. He was the only black cat in the litter and for some reason he looked very much like the tomcat at the end of the street. In addition he had a runny nose and sneezed quite frequently. He was allergic to dust.

"Bashful was the runt of the litter and was always the last to find a nipple for feeding. Fortunately Toots had eight nipples, so there were enough for all the kittens.

"Dopey never made a sound. He didn't mew and he didn't purr. Sleepy of course slept more than the other kittens. Happy was always playing and Grumpy was always complaining and mewing.

"That left Doc. He was the leader and the other kittens used to follow him."

"Did he wear glasses on his nose like the cartoon?" Amanda asked.

The Keyhole

TC ignored the question and continued with his story: "From October to May, we used a coal-fired furnace to heat our home. It was located down the basement in a furnace room and it was my job to shovel coal three times a day to keep the fire going. The coal was located in a separate coal-bin near the furnace.

"Well, as you know, Toots had her basket in the basement near the furnace room and that was where she raised her baby kittens. It was always nice and warm.

"The kittens were just learning how to walk and they would climb out of the basket, and then walk unsteadily around the basement. Toots was usually with them to supervise and pick them up by the scruff of the neck and stand them upright if they fell. It was difficult keeping track of seven small kittens. Bashful was always the last to get out of the basket and stayed close to Toots, while Sneezy was always wandering off on his own.

"One day Sneezy went missing. He was about eight weeks old at the time and was just learning to walk. We searched the basement. We could not find Sneezy anywhere. Toots was not much help. By the eighth week her maternal instinct had disappeared. The kittens were weaned and on their own. Doc, Happy, Sleepy and Dopey had been adopted and only Bashful and Sneezy remained at home with Toots in the basket. Toots spent most of the day out and about, looking for mice and sleeping upstairs. As far as she was concerned, Sneezy might have been adopted. She didn't miss him.

"We looked all over for Sneezy. We checked out every corner of the basement and every room. We even looked in the furnace room. There was a door in the basement that opened to the outside, so we expanded our search to our property and the neighbouring properties. There was still no sign of Sneezy. A day passed, then a second day. We posted a lost kitten ad at the corner store and I checked with all of the neighbours. There was still no sign of Sneezy; I had given up.

"Toots, however, was acting strangely. She would approach me with her tail held high signaling friendship. Then she would mew a few times, turn and go down the basement. Toots was trying to tell me something. She did this several times and I finally decided to follow her down the stairs to her basket. Toots didn't stop there. She wanted me to follow her and headed for the furnace room. Then she sat in front of the coal storage room and started to mew. That is when I heard a sneeze coming from inside the room.

"I looked in the coal storage room and there was Sneezy. He was thin, dirty and blacker than black. He was covered with coal dust and too weak to stand up. Toots' maternal instinct took over and she jumped up on the pile of coal, grabbed Sneezy by the scruff of the neck and carried him back to her basket. I filled up Toots' bowl with fresh water and returned to find Toots licking the coal dust from Sneeze's dirty fur."

"So what happened to Sneezy and Bashful?" Amanda asked. "Did anyone adopt them?"

"They were both adopted, Amanda. Bashful was adopted by a librarian who thought that he would be a good companion. Sneezy was adopted by a doctor who was interested in allergies."

"Did he cure Sneezy?"

"As a matter of fact he did," TC replied. "He found out that Sneezy had a sinus infection and he was able to cure it."

Amanda got up from her stool and stretched.

"I liked that memory, TC; it had a very happy ending."

35
Catnaps

"Cats can work out mathematically the exact place to sit that will cause the most inconvenience."
— *Pam Brown*

"TC, when I looked through the keyhole I could see Toots and she was sleeping in a washbasin. What was she doing there?"

"Pull up a step, Amanda, and I will tell you all about Toots, her cat naps, her cat dreams and her two favourite places to sleep.

"Cats are not like you and me. They spend three quarters of their life sleeping. They are masters in the art of sleeping. They can drape themselves over the stuffed arms of a chair, snuggle up to a pillow, curl up into a ball on the floor or stretch out flat on their back on a comfortable rug. They snore, they chatter and they mumble. They twist and turn, their whiskers twitch and their paws reach out for imagined prey. They are just as unpredictable as we are when asleep."

"Do cats dream like you and I, TC?"

"We do not know for sure, but I think the answer is yes. Cats have good memories. Once they learn to do something, they never forget it. They remember good experiences and bad experiences. Our brains work the same way. We store those memories in our brains all of our life and when we go to sleep some of those memories will come back to us in the form of a dream. Sometimes the events are not properly connected and we will wake up saying, 'I just had the craziest dream.'

"Sometimes it will be a frightening dream when your imagination gets involved. When I was your age, Amanda, I used to have nightmares and wake up screaming. At other times I would be in an imaginary fight or trying to escape and then I would fall out of bed."

"I would have liked to see you fall out of bed, TC," Amanda laughed.

"Well, cats are just like us," TC continued. "You can see their paws moving or they may tense up ready to pounce while reliving a mouse event. Sometimes they will hiss with tail down, remembering a fight with a neighbouring cat who had invaded their territory."

"TC, you have been telling me all about sleeping and dreaming, but you have not told me why Toots was sleeping in the washbasin."

"I left that to the last, Amanda, because I really do not know. Many cats sleep in sinks or washbasins. Toots was not alone. Cats usually have two or three favourite sleeping places. Toots had only two, her basket and the washbasin. I think that she liked the basin because she could fit in nicely and it was up high so she would be safe. Since cats have a thick coat of fur, they do not need a soft surface to sleep, but they do like a surface that is cool. The basin was both smooth and cool."

Amanda laughed.

"I guess she was just having a catnap."

36
Merry Christmas

"On the second day of Christmas
My true love sent to me
Two turtle doves
And a partridge in a pear tree."
– The Twelve Days of Christmas Carol

"TC, I looked through the keyhole and your Christmas tree had fallen on the floor and you were cleaning up the mess. How did the tree fall over?"

"You had better ask Toots," TC laughed. "She knocked over the tree."

"What do you mean," Amanda asked.

"Just give me a minute, Amanda, and I will tell you all about that memory. It is one of my favourites."

TC had a coughing spell and took a few minutes to catch his breath before settling into his rocking chair. He offered Amanda a cough candy and popped one in his own mouth. The memory story began.

The Keyhole

"It was the day before Christmas. We always cut our own tree at that time. It was usually a spruce tree and there was a conservation area within the city limits that allowed you to cut trees. It was out on the islands at the mouth of the Kam River and was only a twenty-minute run from our house. The trees that you could cut were all tagged. But the nice thing was they were free. My dad would load up the car with an axe, a small swede saw and some rope to tie the tree down to the roof of the car.

"We arrived at the site and then headed into the bush to find the perfect tree. That was always a problem because each of us had a different idea about perfection. My mother liked short and bushy, my sister liked tall and slim, I liked a bushy bottom and a nice taper to a medium height. My father said that he really didn't care . . . just get on with it. Eventually, with a little bit of compromising, we settled on a tree that satisfied most of our qualifications.

"The tree was duly chopped down and we were quite surprised at its size. When you are outdoors trees appear to be smaller than they really are. This tree was obviously too big, so we made the first amputation with the swede saw and cut off about 30 cm. Then we dragged the tree out to the car and were quite surprised when my dad, who had not been with us during the selection and harvesting operation, announced that the tree was much too big to carry on the roof of the car. A second amputation with the swede saw reduced the length by another 30 cm. We tied the tree to the roof of the car and headed home.

"We arrived home with our trophy tree and were quite surprised when my grandmother came out of the house; she took one look at the tree and announced that it would never fit inside the house. It was not only too high but it was too bushy. So we removed an additional 30 cm from the tree and pruned back the lower branches, which originally had been a compromise for mother's bushy condition. A wood base shaped like a cross was then nailed to the bottom of the tree and we carried our amputee patient indoors.

"When we tilted the tree upright it was evident that the top leader of the fir tree bent over when it hit the ceiling. So we then cut off another 10 cm to make it fit. We also pruned back some more of the lower branches, which were hitting an adjacent armchair. Both the armchair and the adjacent couch were out of bounds for Toot since she liked to scratch the upholstery. The tree was now thinner and 1m shorter.

"Since the tree was not perfectly straight, we put a wedge under the wood base so that it appeared to be upright. My mother had all of the decorations from the previous year ready. They had been packed away in boxes and stored in the basement. We started to decorate.

"The first job was to get the lights to work. These were old strings and if one light burned out all of the remaining lights on the string went out. Dad was in charge of the lights and after much cursing and prayers to whichever god was in charge of lighting he got the first string to work. The second and third strings were easier and the cursing was not as loud or as frequent. Fortunately Grandma was slightly deaf and did not hear. She read her bible every night and definitely did not approve of swearing. Dad's remarkable vocabulary was not acceptable to her.

"After the lights were strung, we applied tinsel made from aluminized paper to simulate icicles hanging from the tree. Toots always sat and watched the decorating. She liked tinsel. She could bat it with her paw. The glass balls went on next.

With the experience gained from past ball attacks and breakage, we put them high enough so that Toots could not reach them. A few strings of popcorn were added and the tree was finished. At least we thought it was finished until mom removed the wrapper from the forgotten star of Bethlehem. Since the star had to go on the top of the tree, another 10cm was lopped off, so that the total amputation now exceeded 1m."

"Why didn't you just get a measuring tape when you went out to cut the tree?" Amanda asked.

"Good point, Amanda. I guess we never learned our lesson, because every year it was the same procedure. However, that year we set a record.

"We were all sitting back admiring the tree when my sister came in with two turtle doves. They had feathers and were quite realistic and represented the two turtle doves in the *Christmas Carol*. She had saved and bought them with her own money. I suggested that she could have saved money by buying just one partridge. She just ignored me and placed the doves in a prominent spot, near the top of the tree. Toots had been sitting by, watching the decorating and she was very interested in the birds. The doves looked quite real to her, except they didn't move and they didn't make a sound.

"We finished off the day with a glass of mulled cider to celebrate our tree decorating project and then hung up our socks for Santa's arrival. Toots just kept watching the doves and secretly planned her next move. We all retired for the night, pleased with our creativity and looking forward to the Christmas Day ahead.

"Toots did not retire. She wanted to catch those doves. When it was dark she crept from her basket and went upstairs. Cats cannot see when it is completely dark, but when there is a little light they can see quite well. The hall light beside the living room was on. She could see quite clearly. The doves were still on the Christmas tree, silent and motionless. Toots crept slowly with her belly close to the carpet in her best hunting form. She jumped onto the forbidden sofa, paused and then jumped again onto the tree and grabbed one of the doves. The Christmas tree came crashing down and Toots ran off with the dove. The house was silent.

"The next morning, I was the first one up, discovered the mess and started to clean it up. We all thought that the tree had fallen over on its own. My dad thought it was the wedge that we had used. That is the memory that you saw through the keyhole."

"So how did you find out it was Toots?"

"Later on I found the dove in my boot. It was a gift. I guess that it was Toots' way of wishing me a Merry Christmas!"

37
Cat Talk

"If cats could talk, they wouldn't."
— Nan Porter

Amanda was in the barn and had her ear to the keyhole. She thought that she had heard a sound inside the room. It had sounded like a cat mewing. She looked through the keyhole and the room was dark, but there was enough light that she could see Toots sitting beside the back door. She was looking up at the door knob, knowing that if the knob turned, there was someone on the other side who was going to open the door and let her in. Amanda put her ear to the keyhole again. There was no further sound. She must have imagined it. The knob turned, the door opened and TC let Toots in the house. Amanda reported this event to TC when they next met.

"I thought that I heard a sound in your memory room when I was out in the barn," Amanda announced. "It sounded like a cat mewing."

TC shook his head. "A memory is like a dream, Amanda. There is no sound. It is just like a silent movie. You must have imagined hearing a sound."

Amanda was not convinced but continued the conversation. She was sure that she had heard Toots mewing to get in the house.

"Can cats talk, TC? Is mewing or purring, their way of talking?"

"In answer to your first question, Amanda, yes cats do talk. In answer to your second question, yes mewing and purring are two ways in which cats talk, but they have many other ways of communicating. Let me explain.

"Cat language is made up of a combination of body movements, scent signals and sounds. We are aware of the sounds like yowls, hisses, growls, mews and purrs, but we miss the other signals."

"What do you mean?" Amanda asked.

"Well you should watch a cat's tail to see what she wants to tell you. If you wake up and the cat greets you with its tail held straight up it means 'Good morning, I'm glad to be with you'. On the other hand if the tail is wagging it means stay away.

"Toots was usually afraid whenever she saw a dog and she would tuck her tail between her legs. If she was cornered she would crouch low, with ears slicked back and hiss or growl. If she was terrified she would roll over on her back, not as a sign of submission but because she wanted to have all four paws, claws extended, ready to defend herself."

"That would be very confusing, TC. The dog might think this was a sign of submission."

"Cats never submit, Amanda. But let me continue. There are other ways that cats talk. For instance, they can talk with their eyes. Any strong emotion such as fear, pleasure anger or excitement will cause the cat's pupil to narrow into a slit. A bowl of her favourite food or a gift of catnip makes this happen.

"When Toots' eyes were wide open, you knew that she trusted you. Her eyes were very precious and if there was any sign of danger she would protect herself by narrowing them to a slit.

"Cats also talk by smelling or scratching. They have scent pads between their toes in the pads of their feet and scratching leaves some of this scent. They have signaled their ownership and marked their territory.

"Cats have similar scent glands in other parts of their body and rubbing or bunting against other animal or people leaves this scent and again signifies acceptance into her family and territory. It was a compliment when Toots rubbed against my leg."

"What about purring?"

"Cats do communicate by purring," TC replied. "They usually will not purr when they are alone, but they do purr when they meet other cats or people. Toots purred to her kittens to reassure them that they were safe and that she had a supply of milk for them to drink. The kittens would purr in return, signaling their contentment. Toots and her kittens were talking to each other."

Amanda smiled. "I think that a purr is like a smile and that I was just talking to you."

TC smiled in return, but Amanda continued: "The thing that I like about you, TC, is that we can have heart to heart talks with each other. It is often difficult for me to talk to my mom and my dad or my teacher, but you make it easy."

TC wiped a tear from his eye. "Sharing my memories with you has brought great joy to my life, Amanda. Thank you."

38
Pinched

"The world is my lobster."
– Henry J. Tillman

Amanda and TC were having one of their many discussions sitting on the front porch.

"I was looking through the keyhole and saw Toots in a big laundry tub. She had her paws up on the edge of the tub, but couldn't get out," Amanda reported.

"Well as you know Toots was a very curious cat. She was interested in anything that moved, and she liked to eat fish. She was down the basement one day and her hunting instinct told her that there was something moving in the laundry tub and it smelled fishy. Toots decided to investigate. She jumped up on a chair beside the tub and looked over the edge and saw some strange creatures that smelled fishy but they didn't look like fish. They had big claws, eight legs and a tail. They had big bulging eyes that stuck out from their head. They looked like monsters from another planet. They were lobsters. They were all moving around with one on top of the other. Toots was confused. She had never seen, never caught and never eaten a lobster. This was something new. She looked in the tub and studied the lobsters for a long time."

"How did the lobsters get in the laundry tub, TC?"

"Well my dad put them there. Let me tell you a little bit about our family history. Our ancestors came from Kilkeel, Ireland in the 1800s and settled in Lorneville, New Brunswick. They earned their living fishing for cod and salmon in the Bay of Fundy. Lobsters that were pulled up in their nets were usually thrown back in the ocean. Some were taken home and cooked but they were considered to be a poor man's food. At school one peanut butter and jelly sandwich was a fair trade for two lobster sandwiches.

"As time passed, the cod were fished out and the fishermen decided to harvest lobster using wooden traps baited with fish and with openings which allowed the lobster to enter, but not escape. Lobster was originally only eaten by people who lived by the sea but as it became more popular, it was refrigerated using ice and was shipped to nearby locations by train."

"So how did the lobster get to your home? Fort William was a long way from the ocean."

"Well there was a fish store in New Brunswick, owned by one of our cousins and they would pack the live lobster in wooden barrels filled with ice and seaweed. Then they would ship the barrels by train to our home in Fort William. It took about four days to get there. When the barrels arrived my dad would pick them up, take them home and then unpack them, hoping the lobsters were still alive. The only place that he could think of putting the lobsters was in the laundry tub in the basement. He didn't tell my mother. She would have been horrified, but since she never did the laundry or looked in the tub, she did not have to know. My grandmother and my sister were away at the time. My dad swore our maid Lena and me to secrecy.

"Lena and I then added some ice and seaweed to the tub so that the lobsters would survive for a few more days. Freshwater could not be added or the lobsters would die. They require salt water.

"The lobster would miraculously appear cooked on our table the next day with the simple explanation that, Lena got them. That was not a lie. The words from the laundry tub in the basement were conveniently left out. I think that my mother really knew what was going on, but she went along with the charade because she really loved to eat lobster."

"Did you like eating the lobster, TC?"

"Not in the beginning, Amanda, but in time I became very fond of it. My family was really into seafood. Only one half of a lobster is actually edible. You only eat meat from the tail and the claws. There is also some meat in the legs, but it is hard to get out.

"Let me continue my story. Toots looked down and studied the lobster for a long time. She was fascinated. They all had rubber bands around their claws so that they couldn't eat each other and also so we could handle them without getting pinched.

"Toots had tried to swipe at the lobsters with one paw but the tub was too deep and she couldn't reach them. Finally she ran out of patience. She decided to catch one of the lobsters and jumped into the tub. Unknown to Toots, one of the lobsters had lost its rubber band in shipment. This was the lobster that she had picked.

"That was a mistake. Toots usually bit the neck off her catch to break it, but this creature didn't have a neck. So she tried unsuccessfully to bite the tail. The shell was too hard. The lobster in the meantime was starving after its long trip from the ocean and pinched the only thing in sight with its free claw. It was wormlike waving in front of him. It looked edible. It was Toots' tail.

"Toots turned to attack the lobster but as she turned she dragged the lobster with her. She couldn't reach the vulnerable head and couldn't bite into the hard shell of the upper body. The lobster in the meantime would not let go of her tail. Toots tried to jump out of the tub but could not get out with the lobster hanging on. So she just stood with her paws on the edge of the tub and mewed for help.

"That is the memory that you saw, Amanda, when you looked through the keyhole."

"Did someone recue Toots?" Amanda asked.

"Yes, I came home from school and found Toots in the basement with the lobster still hanging on to her tail. The lobster would not let go, so I got a knife and cut the claw off. Her tail was free. Toots jumped out of the laundry tub, ran and hid in her basket."

"Did Toots like to eat lobster, TC?"

"Of course, Amanda, I cracked the severed claw and gave the meat to Toots."

39
Home! Sweet Home!

"Mid pleasures and palaces though we may roam,
Be it ever so humble there's no place like home;
A charm from the skies seems to hallow us there,
Which seek thro' the world, is ne'er met elsewhere.
Home! Home!
Sweet, sweet home!
There's no place like home
There's no place like home!"
– John Howard Payne – 1823

"TC, I looked through the keyhole and I saw Toots sitting on the window sill again. It was just like the first memory story, only this time Toots looked quite old and half of one ear was missing. She looked cold and wanted to get in the house.""Okay, Amanda, I will tell you about that memory. But first, let's go in the house. I find it is a little too chilly for me out on the front porch."

TC got up slowly from his rocking chair with the help of his cane. Amanda opened the front door and they went inside. The passage of time on TC's road of life had taken its toll. He was always lean, but had grown thinner. Once tall he was now bent over, but not broken. An age-ravaged face had replaced a once unblemished boyish countenance. A streaked shock of white on brown hair had replaced the hair, once blonde. He shuffled forward and slowly eased into his favourite chair. His briar pipe and pipe rack, once a fixture, had been put away.

TC started to cough. His coughing had become persistent and he held a handkerchief to his mouth to catch the blood flecked phlegm.

"Give me a minute, Amanda. I'll be okay."

Amanda waited for TC to tell the story. TC seemed to have recovered.

"So what was Toots doing on the window sill and what happened to her ear?" Amanda asked.

TC picked up the story line. "As you know, Amanda, we had a summer cottage at Amethyst Harbour on Lake Superior. The cottage was about 50 km from our home in Fort William. Toots would spend the summer with us at the cottage and she had a great time hunting for birds and mice, bringing them home and then depositing them in my shoes. I always had to check my shoes when I put them on.

"Toots also liked to wander and explore and sometimes she would disappear for a few days. But she would always return home for a good meal. Summer came to an end and it was time to return to our home in Fort William. School began in early September. We were all packed up, ready to leave and could not find Toots. My dad was waiting in the car and was anxious to get going. We knew that Toots did not like driving in the car and I thought that she was probably hiding. I checked under the beds, inside the woodshed and all of her favourite places. No Toots!

After one hour, dad had run out of patience and brought the search to an end by announcing that we were going home and leaving Toots.

"I was heartbroken and cried all the way home. By that time my dad's blood pressure had returned to normal and he assured me that we would drive back the next weekend and look for Toots. I was not to worry, but I worried all week."

"So did you go back and find Toots?" Amanda asked.

"Yes we did go back to our cottage at Amethyst, not only that next weekend, but also the following weekend. There was still no Toots. It was on the second weekend, when we were closing up the cottage for the winter, that my dad announced: 'We are not coming back. Toots is gone. She may have got run over by a car or killed by the coyotes. We will never know. Cats can be replaced. I will buy you another cat.'

"I started to cry and pleaded that Toots had probably gone off on one of her trips. Maybe she was visiting another family. But it was no use. My dad would not change his mind.

"I cried all the way home. If Toots was gone I did not want another cat. No cat could ever replace Toots. The months passed. Christmas and the New Year followed. Toots had become an all but forgotten memory.

"It was a Saturday morning in January and as usual it was bitterly cold. The milk bottles on the back steps had popped their caps and the cream had squeezed out of the bottle like toothpaste.

"Then Toots appeared! She was sitting there on our windowsill in her favourite spot, all huddled up with half her ear missing, shivering and mewing to get in from the cold.

"Toots had spent the past three months on an incredible fifty kilometre journey from our cottage in Amethyst to our home in

Fort William. We did not know how she did it. The only connecting link was a highway and a railway track. She had to find her way, not only through our city but also through the neighbouring city of Port Arthur.

"I thought that she had probably used the railroad track because it was close to our cottage at Amethyst and it also passed close to our home in Fort William. But even that route was difficult with many confusing spur lines and railway yards. In addition there was always the constant freight and passenger traffic travelling both east and west. Marauding coyotes and foxes were also a danger on this miraculous journey home.

"When I found Toots, I gathered her in my arms and hugged her. She had no strength and had probably lost half of her original weight. My grandmother warmed a bowl of milk and some leftover porridge. Even my dad had a tear in his eye and announced: 'Toots has a home with us forever. We will never leave her again.'"

"Wow! That was a great story, TC. I guess that Toots had decided that there's no place like home."

"That is correct, Amanda. It is just like the old song teaches us.

"Be it ever so humble, there's no place like home."

40
Nine Lives

"The cat has nine lives, three for playing,
three for straying, and three for staying."
— Anon

Amanda was on the front porch counting on her fingers.

"TC, I just figured out that Toots must have been with you for a long time because she has only used up five of her nine lives in the memories that you have told me. She has four lives left."

"How did you figure that out?" TC asked.

"Well she came home from your cottage at Amethyst Harbour and she came back from Kakabeka Falls. Both times you thought that she was dead. Next she fell down the hole at the Amethyst mine. Then she got locked in the attic and almost starved and finally she almost drowned in the river. So that leaves four."

"Well the saying that a cat has nine lives is just a superstition, Amanda. People believe in this superstition because cats can survive falls from high places with few, if any injuries. This gives the appearance that the cat has come back to life.

"I think the ability of the cat to survive accidents, that might kill you and I, is not due to multiple lives but to several advantages that they possess. Their small size and low body weight softens the impact when they hit the ground after falling from great heights."

"Okay, that would be like when she fell down the shaft at the Amethyst mine. That was pretty high," Amanda remarked.

"Yes it was," TC replied. "But cats have other advantages that we do not have. They have highly developed inner ears that give them a very good sense of balance, which helps them to land on their feet. Even if a cat is falling upside down it is able to right itself by rapidly determining where it is, so that it can make any adjustments necessary to make sure that it lands on all four feet. If you and I were falling upside down, that is probably the way that we would land."

"Not me," said Amanda. "I would just put my arms out and fly like Supergirl."

TC chuckled and then continued: "Now, let me finish. Since cats land on all four paws the impact from landing is absorbed by all four. Additionally cats can bend their legs when they land, which cushions the impact by spreading the force not through the bones that can easily break but through the joints and muscles as well.

"The most interesting thing is that a cat which falls from a high place has a better chance of survival than a cat which falls from a low place. We know that an object with a large area will fall slower than an object with a small area. That is why parachutes that are open are considerably better than parachutes that fail to open. When a cat is falling it spreads its legs into a parachute shape, which slows the fall. Height provides more time for the cat to get organized."

"So my Supergirl idea would work," Amanda remarked. "Now tell me, TC. If Toots didn't have nine lives, how long did she live?"

TC paused thinking back in time.

"Well, when I was growing up most indoor house cats lived for fifteen years and the outdoor cats lived for five years. Toots lived for almost ten years because she was mostly an indoor cat."

"Did she go to heaven?" Amanda asked. "Did you feel bad?"

"Well she did not go to heaven because there is no heaven for cats," TC replied.

"Heaven is something that some humans believe in. It is part of their religious beliefs."

"Did you bury Toots?"

"Yes I did. I buried Toots out in the backyard in the same spot that I had buried all of the dead mice and birds that she had brought home. I thought that she would be happier there."

41
Goodbye

My Grandfather's clock
Was too large for the shelf,
So it stood ninety years on the floor;
It was taller by half
Than the old man himself,
Though it weighed not a pennyweight more;
It was bought on the morn
Of the day he was born,
It was always his treasure and pride;

But it stopped short Never to go again, When the old man died. Ninety years without slumbering, Tick, tock, tick, tock, His life seconds numbering, Tick, tock, tick, tock, It stopped short, Never to go again, When the old man died.

– Henry Clay Work – 1876

Amanda was home early. She dumped her back-pack at the house and walked to the barn. There was no light coming from the keyhole. That was strange. Amanda bent over so that she could look through the keyhole. It was dark inside.

Amanda was upset. She ran to the house yelling, "TC! TC! Your room is dark."

She couldn't find TC. But her mother was home unusually early, so she asked her.

"Mom, I can't find TC. Where is he?"

"Sit down, Amanda, and I will tell you what has happened.

"TC has left us. He died while you were at school. He just went to sleep and never woke up. He was ninety years old and had lived a full life. Today was his birthday.

"Here is a letter which he left. It has your name on it."

Amanda tried, but could not hold back the tears. This was her first experience with death. She could not imagine that TC was gone forever. There would be no more stories about Toots. No more stories about TC growing up. No more of those crazy adventures. Amanda tried to swallow. There was a big lump in her throat and the tears would not stop. It was hard, really hard.

Amanda reached for her mother's outstretched arms.

"He was a good Grandpa, Amanda. He really loved you."

Then she handed Amanda the letter. Amanda opened the envelope. There was a rusty old key and a note inside.

Dear Amanda,

The reason that you can no longer see a light in my room is that I have taken my memories with me. The room is now empty, but I have left you my key so that you can store your memories in the room. Maybe someday you will have a granddaughter to share them with. Our time together has brought me great joy, Amanda. I hope that you have enjoyed the adventures of Toots. I love you truly.

TC

Amanda folded the letter and put the key in her pocket. As she left the living room, she glanced at the grandfather clock. It had stopped short, never to go again.

Afterword

My friends and family nicknamed me TC. My father was always called ST. Initial names are a family thing. Most of this story is based on events that happened when I was growing up in the 1930s at our family home in Fort William, Ontario. We had a cat named Toots and most of the adventures that I relate about Toots and my friends are true. However, I do confess that I have borrowed from the lives of other cats that I have met and are owned by family and friends. I also confess that much of this story has been invented. Writers are allowed to do that, when creating a novel.

My sister, Mugs has always claimed that Toots was her cat. That sibling dispute remains unresolved. I did, however, dedicate the book to her.

Chapter 39 is, however, true. Toots did indeed make the incredible journey from our cottage at Amethyst to our home in Fort William. The story of Toots was also an inspiration to others, including a family friend named, Sheila Burnford. She wrote her version of the story, titled *The Incredible Journey*, about a cat and two dogs that make a similar long distance trek through insurmountable obstacles. The book became a best seller and a Hollywood movie.

I have tried to make alternate chapters in the book a life learning experience for young readers. As older adults we are all stakeholders and mentors in the future lives of not only our children, but also our grandchildren. We can build a learning foundation and light the spark in the minds of this future generation. Of course, I have also written all of the chapters for the many members of our society who are cat lovers and enjoy reading about cats.

It was great fun writing the novel. Many years ago my wife Shirley and I were spending a winter in Bermuda. It is a rather small island and after a month, I had run out of places to explore and things to do. I did not golf, fish or hike. Tourists could not rent cars, only mopeds. I was bored. Shirley suggested that I should spend my time writing my memoires. I accepted the challenge and for the next month I kept myself busy writing down recollections of various events that had occurred during my boyhood. I created about fifty short pieces and then put them away and did not look at them for the next ten years.

After spending three years writing and publishing a historical novel about diamonds, I needed a change of scene. My journalist daughter Colleen Isherwood had reviewed the Bermuda articles and suggested that I could use some of the material for a novel. So here it is: *The Keyhole*. I hope that you read, learn and enjoy the adventures of Toots the cat!

Acknowledgements

I would like to thank Colleen Isherwood, editor of *Canadian Lodging News* for reviewing the manuscript at various stages of development. I also appreciate the tolerance of my wife Shirley, who politely listened and criticized each chapter as they were produced.

I of course always give credit to my high school English teacher Christine Tilden for counseling me to pursue a career in journalism rather than a career in engineering. It is ironic that after a successful fifty-year career in engineering, I should follow her advice. I wish that she were here to share my stories.

I would also like to give credit to my friend Richard Dewey, who despite his allergic relationship with cats, created the cover image for this book.

I would also like to thank Ida and David Warren for providing the photograph of their cat Johanne which appears on the front cover image.

Thanks also to the staff at FriesenPress for their patience and counsel in reviewing, publishing and marketing *The Keyhole*.

Bibliography

Burnford, Sheila. *The Incredible Journey*

O'Neill, Amanda. *The Complete Book of the Cat*

Snopek, Roxanne Willems. *More Great Cat Stories*

Wright, Michael & Walters, Sally. *The Book of the Cat*